THE HIDDEN EYE

*Dedicated to
Livia Sbarbaro*

... however much you deny the truth, the truth goes on existing, as it were, behind your back.

George Orwell

CHAPTER 1

February, 2024

The late afternoon light flooded the distant shoreline of the Wirral, bathing the many buildings that sat along the edge of the land with a golden yellow. The river had sweated a fine grey mist that lingered across its breadth, thick and low. Strangely, as if by magic, it appeared to disperse along its length. Kate Nolan stood on the small balcony, their new balcony, her hands resting on the cold upper steel of the glazed edge. Tim stood just behind, feeling her warmth, her happiness oozed with it.

Pointing, she fixed her eyes on the lighthouse at New Brighton. Despite looking small from this distance, she knew its dimensions well.

'Never in my wildest dreams did I ever think I'd live facing this beautiful river.' Turning, she pulled Tim closer. 'We,' she swiftly corrected.

He said nothing in reply but turned her back round to admire the view as an easyJet aeroplane came into view, a vivid splash of bright orange and white, a contrast against the pewter skyline. Slowly, it climbed away from the city, grey vapour leaching from each wingtip in sharp, parallel streaks, growing darker and stronger until it was swiftly swallowed in the cloud layer. The lines remained briefly before they, too, disappeared. The crackle of the engines followed immediately. He picked up a bottle of Prosecco from a plastic bucket before pulling a face. 'Improvisation until we …' He did not finish but twisted the top and poured two mugs, another compromise. 'To our new home.' He raised his mug. 'I love you, Kate.'

There was a dull sound of the mugs touching. She stood on tiptoe and kissed him. 'We'll soon be straight, and this apartment will become a home, our home.'

CHAPTER 2

Spring 2024

Kate woke earlier than usual, feeling strangely alert, even after a fitful night. Sleep would continue to be a stranger to her, and she realised there was no point in further resistance. She could neither blame Tim's loud snoring nor the cheese she had eaten the previous evening. The midnight indigestion had been remedied, but she had still found sleep a challenge. She tugged the disappearing quilt from under her chin and yawned. Following up on the original idea – a challenge, she believed – would be a mere bagatelle for someone who could balance most of life's challenges with little difficulty. Keeping it a secret had proved to be the fly in the ointment. Why could things not just run smoothly? She had enough on her plate with work demanding more of her time, including requesting her presence on a Saturday.

Her mind was full, a jumble of tasks to finalise in preparation for the holiday, the first they would take together as a couple. Initially, they had met in Ibiza. It had been towards the end of the fortnight when they had stumbled together in an alcohol-induced haze. Tim had immediately appealed to her: his laughter, his humour and she had to admit, his body. On returning, she had often joked with her mates that it had been a long way to go to meet and shag a guy from her home city. An exchange of numbers meant they met again soon after their return and although they initially seemed very different in both personality and outlook, there was an immediate chemistry. Added to this was an unusual mutual attraction – a strong work ethic – and he was good in bed. Tim had turned out to be just as she had anticipated. He was what she had needed to put her life on a steady track. The icing on the cake was that her mother liked him, too, and that could not be said for many of the boys she had previously brought home.

The room was dark, other than for the light blue glow from the bedside clock. She tried to organise the tasks she had set herself, prioritising her check list chronologically against working around her professional commitments. *Why was there never enough time? Why had she decided to plan it in the first place? Why surprise him? It was neither his birthday nor any kind of anniversary and if she were honest, she or they couldn't afford the time away.* The thoughts tumbled in her head bringing more frustration and an inability to sleep.

Slipping from the bed, she grabbed her dressing gown, tied the dressing gown cord and stared at Tim with envy. His mouth was slightly agape, his body curled, almost foetal in its position. 'You're worth the effort, you beautiful man,' she whispered before heading for the kitchen. Coffee would solve everything, help put the confused jigsaw of tasks into a manageable order. She stole a glance through the vertical blinds. The river, the Mersey, looked wide and dark through the floor-to-ceiling apartment window. Myriad lights were still reflected along its length, dancing and shimmering across its ever-moving surface like multi-coloured wisps. She watched as the flashes of light fractured before swiftly, and only briefly, becoming whole again. She could almost sense the strength of the wind blowing along the broad expanse of water by the intensity of the fulminating reflecting filaments. It made her shiver.

Sitting at the table as the dawn broke, she finalised her agenda. The list was soon tucked into her dressing gown pocket and another two coffees were prepared. Saturday and he could sleep in. It was just after eight when the coffee was placed on his bedside table. She kissed him.

'The beautiful, stunning princess wakes the handsome, snoring, dribbling prince, with a kiss and a coffee.' Her loose, blonde hair touched his face as she pulled away.

His fingers came immediately to his nose, and he rubbed it before both hands found his eyes. Further rubbing ensued.

'Time, is it?' Tim's eyes remained only partially open, his voice, strained. He yawned.

'Charming! I'm wasted on you, Tim Foxton, bloody wasted. Your coffee is there.'

Opening his eyes fully he smiled and collected the mug. 'Ta, Babe. Love you!'

Kate sighed. 'I love your snores, grunts and warm morning words. You know I'm working today unlike some folk who are close enough to be poked with a thick stick. I've got jobs to do. You, my man, can prepare a meal this evening for when I come home.'

'Beans on toast it is then?' He sipped his coffee, his sly grin hidden by the rim of the mug as he waited for the fusillade of words to come back, increasing in velocity. He was wrong and if honest, rather disappointed.

Kate disappeared into the bathroom after forcefully closing the bedroom door. Within fifteen minutes, she was standing in front of the wardrobe, running her hand along the clothing. She selected a trouser suit, a grey blouse and black, flat shoes. Pausing, she stopped at the tie rack hanging on the back of the door. Tim had a passion for ties. She lifted her favourite, a deep blue with a fine pin stripe of yellow. It brought a smile. She smelled it and the aroma she knew so well, his aftershave, filled her nostrils.

Tim was at the table demolishing a large bowl of Frosties.

'Tonight, my handsome man, the meal will be imaginative – check. The wine, red – check. Music, romantic – check. Sex, if everything else is in place, exciting – check and literally … mate.' She announced all this in short, sharp demands, her face never slipping from serious. He saluted as she walked over, kissed him on the forehead and turned to leave. 'Love you.'

'Love you, too. Orders received and clearly understo…' The door closed. Collecting the packet, he poured more cereal.

CHAPTER 3

The solicitor's office had been unusually busy, but the morning had flown by. Checking her watch, it was just before one, Kate consulted the list: cash machine followed by the travel agent's. The money was hers, a winning month on the Premium Bonds, five prizes totalling £2,775 had come as a total, yet welcome surprise. She had been desperate to tell Tim but then the idea for the holiday came to her. What better way to tell him than presenting the tickets, after all, it was not really their money, it was hers.

Rob Duncan dropped two files into her in-tray as she was getting ready to leave. Kate knew that he harboured a soft spot for her. They had been friends for some time, and he had brought her into the firm.

'Lunch with Tim?' There was a hint of jealousy in his question but nothing hurtful.

Kate raised her eyebrows. 'Not exactly. A clandestine mission but I can't say any more than that. Must dash. Do you want a sandwich collecting?'

He shook his head. 'If those could be sorted on your return?' He pointed to the files, 'I'd be grateful, Miss Bond.' He put two fingers to his lips and pretended to blow the smoke from the barrel of an imaginary gun.

Kate chuckled and left whilst touching her nose and winking.

* * *

The £250 she had just removed from the ATM was added to the £250 she already had. Opening her purse, she slipped the money to the bottom of her bag, placing the strap over her head. Before moving away, she checked both up and down the pavement. It was busy with lunchtime pedestrians. In five minutes, she would be at the Travel Agent's, she would then grab a meal deal from Boots and head back to the office. She was another step closer to ticking more items from the list.

* * *

The lone electric motorbike had been stalking for only minutes as the soon-to-be pillion had watched the woman at the ATM. A call had been made and a rendezvous arranged whilst the woman remained in sight. The spotter and passenger was difficult to identify. Wearing black jeans and a black raised hoody over a black balaclava that left only circles for his eyes, he followed Kate whilst remaining in communication with his accomplice. The bike appeared, pulling up on Paradise Street. The passenger slipped expertly over the bike seat and pointed at the target who was now waiting to cross Hanover Street. Traffic was busy adding to the background noise.

Even though Kate had pressed the button at the pedestrian crossing, illuminating the 'Wait' signal, she ignored it. She glanced up Hanover Street in an effort to judge the distance between the approaching vehicles. As her focus was elsewhere, she failed to notice the bike approaching silently from behind. The rider kept to the edge of the road, slipping up the inside of the queuing vehicles held at the crossroad lights. Spying a gap in the moving traffic, Kate took three quick steps.

The next action took fewer than fifteen seconds. To some it occurred in the blink of an eye. The bike slipped quickly and neatly onto the pavement, scattering four pedestrians, before immediately following Kate onto Hanover Street. It was all happening so, so quickly. Kate turned at the sound of a shout or scream, but by that time a gloved hand had slipped onto the strap of her bag. The bike accelerated and turned. As if by instinct, she, too, grabbed the strap with her left hand but the force and the speed of the moving bike spun her almost three hundred and sixty degrees, the centrifugal force lifting first one foot and then the other away from the tarmac.

Nigel Chadburn, a passer-by, stood and watched the unfolding robbery. His mouth hung loosely open. He could hardly comprehend what was taking place just in front of him.

* * *

Now totally out of balance, Kate released the strap but still attempted to grab the bag with her other hand in an endeavour to trap it between her arm and body. Her defensive moves proved to be futile. She was now almost horizontal, still spinning and confused as to the direction in which she was travelling. Her mind grew dizzy, her scream piercing the air. The bike swerved. It, too, was thrown off track by the gyrating attached body.

A heavily ladened lorry was level with her flailing torso, but on the opposite side of the road. It was accelerating to beat the traffic lights that had just turned to amber. Kate had released the bag in desperation. The bike began to move at even greater speed between a car and the lorry. She was immediately ejected at an acute angle to land and roll on the road, before finally sliding between the gap of the lorry's front and back wheels. She was unseen by the lorry driver who just wanted to keep going and maintain his momentum.

Had there not been a kerb, she would have slid and tumbled onto the opposite pavement, battered and bruised, but there was, and she paid for it dearly. Her body bounced back in an upright position immediately before the leviathan's four, near-side wheels. She heard a scream, shrill and piercing, it was her own. She vaguely heard the steady, loud, automated beep from the pedestrian crossing – ironically now signalling it was safe to cross. Neither sound fully registered nor helped. Her view was confused, the sounds clearly unrecognisable. A feeling of detachment encompassed her, as if both present and future were out of her control.

* * *

The driver felt only a slight bump as Kate's world went black, her body crushed under the lorry's wheels. He glanced into his left mirror. It was the leg he saw, a twisted leg. He stamped on the brakes. His first fear was that he had collided with a cyclist.

The bus travelling behind the lorry had stopped, as had the cars and so, too, the many pedestrians. Some observers immediately searched for their phones, but many knew from looking at the contorted and deformed figure spewing from the rear of the lorry, there was little chance of her surviving. Blood haemorrhaged profusely from her ears and mouth and strangely seemed to be emerging from the nape of her twisted neck. There was a sudden, unnatural silence. Those who witnessed the accident, those caught in the moment of madness, struggled to believe what had just transpired. The two, black-clad figures on the bike had no idea of what carnage had followed in their wake. They were long gone.

* * *

Nigel stared at the deformed doll that only moments earlier had been a young, vibrant woman who had eagerly skipped impatiently in front of him. It was a scene that would remain with him, haunt and anger him. If only he had acted as the bike passed, if he had stopped her risking a red light, preventing her from crossing … if only. Noticing one person videoing the scene, his impotence turned to anger. Moving towards them he grabbed their phone before slamming it onto the ground.

Nigel ranted, 'How bloody dare you?'

CHAPTER 4

Tim Foxton stared through the window of the apartment. The river still ran as it had always done in the few short months since they had moved in. The view today was no different. It was just an ordinary day but then it was not, it could not be and maybe his days would never be normal again. He felt numb and yet his mind turned with a maelstrom of endless confused words. They played like a stuck record – *She told me she was on a clandestine mission. We joked about it. She said nothing else.* These words ran through his mind like hot steel, bringing nausea, anguish, disbelief – all conspiring to plant a seed of suspicion. They had been written in a statement by her work colleague, a statement made to the police investigating her cruel death. Then there was the withdrawal of money of which he was totally unaware. The Premium Bond win had also been revealed. This bombardment of hidden truths clouded his ability to think straight. The actions were so unlike Kate. He broke down.

'What have you done to me, Kate? What secrets have you kept from me? Why?'

* * *

Two weeks later, Tim watched the gates to Anfield Cemetery from inside the limousine as it followed the hearse. The gothic structure churned his stomach as the reality struck. This was happening. It was real and now, only now, did he realise that his life could never be the same ... his world had been turned upside down, thrown into disarray. For the first time for as long as he could remember, he felt his mother's hand on his. Turning, he saw the love in her eyes, an understanding and with it, a strength.

'I know where your thoughts are. Your mother knows. Always remember she was a good girl, kind and loving. She loved you. I could sense that. You trusted her in life and so you should now trust her in death. Trust your mother, Tim, especially when your thoughts seek the darker corners where the shadows of despair lurk.' As she spoke, she caressed the dark lines beneath his eyes with her small hand. 'She thought the world of you, and she would never do anything to harm you. That I know and that you must always believe.' Removing her hand, she brought it to rest on her lips before returning it to his. He turned away.

Her words seemed like smoke, blending with the others before slowly vanishing into the darkness of his grief. Moving his hand to his throat he adjusted the knot of his tie, her tie, her favourite colours, and he wept again.

'One day soon you will know the truth. On that you must trust me.'

* * *

Rob Duncan was one of the last to enter the chapel. He had watched the many mourners pass through the broad arch from beyond the small circular garden set before the stone chapel. Solemnity seemed to hang heavily. Kate's face swam within his mind's eye. The wink, the smile. Now that mischief would be no more and he felt the loss heavily.

As the last of the line filed in, they found only standing room at the back. 'You'll Never Walk Alone' played through speakers dotted around the chapel. There were no words, just the plaintive cry of strings. For those congregated, the broken and the damaged, the words ran through their minds like tickertape. 'Hold your head up high …' came at the appropriate moment as Rob glanced towards the front, focusing on the coffin and the arrangement of flowers spread along its length. Tim, supported at the front, looked numb and broken, his elder brother stood in the row behind him, a supportive hand on Tim's heavily laden shoulders.

Rob could only reflect that it had taken merely a callous and cruel moment for the precious and special woman to be lost but for those before him, it would take an eternity for that wound and loss to heal; even then, a scar would remain.

He watched as the congregation moved, as if guided by some mysterious hand, back through the archway. He saw Kate's mother, ashen and broken. Her only daughter had been taken too soon. He elected to be the last to leave. The closing of the curtains and the earlier music had made him think of the musical, *Carousel*. It was as if the funeral had been a performance and at any moment the curtains would be drawn back and Kate would reappear, all smiles, bows and bouquets. The heartfelt words of Bruce Springsteen 'If I Should Fall Behind', broke the spell. He knew it was not to be.

* * *

Rob sat at Kate's desk. It seemed an age since she had died, been killed, and yet it was not. The culprits had never been brought to justice. The box containing her personal belongings had been collected days before. He had stared at the framed photograph and reflected on the happier times; Kate and Tim on a beach, all smiles. It had been the last item to be placed in the box. In his solicitor's role, he had often faced grieving relatives, but this was different. It was personal. He had cared deeply for Kate. The fact that he was the last person in the office to chat with her brought a huge burden, as part of that conversation, he knew, had caused a degree of disquiet. However, it had soon been revealed what she had meant by 'clandestine mission'. It had been deciphered and with that, the truth was known, lifting the dark pall of suspicion and uncertainty.

Rob had witnessed the reality as he attended the funeral, he had witnessed the grief and heartache of losing someone so tragically and so young. He felt helpless. His true feelings for her would remain hidden.

CHAPTER 5

Autumn 2024

For Detective Sergeant Skeeter Warlock, walking onto a wrestling mat always brought a flutter of nerves, a tingle of excitement and a degree of trepidation. A brief moment of insecurity was added to the mix – whether that was through uncertainty on seeing her rival, the atmosphere, or her momentary lack of belief in her ability, in her own skill set at that moment, she did not know. What she was certain of was the surge of adrenaline, the increase in her heart rate and the blood flow that she not only craved but loved. They were the stimulants she needed to put her at the top of her game. Walking through the door of Beacon Hill Dental Surgery amalgamated the familiar addictions and emotions of wrestling. It locked them into her stomach, without the thrill and optimism and, most certainly, without the buzz.

She had read about the natural drug adrenaline in the US, known as epinephrine, a hormone and neurotransmitter that helps the body respond to dangerous and stressful conditions, triggering the flight or fight response. Most times she was happy to fight but when the word 'dental' was mentioned, she always felt the desire to turn and run. For a young woman who seemed to declare openly to those who knew her that she was frightened of nothing and nobody, this contradiction, this secret phobia, she kept closely guarded.

She tried to ensure very little of her fear was evident as the chair slowly moved her upper body from vertical to horizontal. She knew by the way her hands gripped the arms of the chair that it was clear she felt uncomfortable.

'Please relax.' The dentist's instruction sounded almost sympathetic.

The words confirmed her suspicion, she had conveyed the signals she had tried so desperately to mask.

'Any problems with your teeth or gums, Skeeter?' The dentist slipped on blue gloves as she spoke, quietly and confidently.

Skeeter shook her head.

'The gum shield we made is obviously doing its job.'

A hand moved to the handle on the side of the lamp that hovered above and drew it closer to Skeeter's face. A finger lifted her upper lip, and another latex-covered finger ran harshly across her teeth and was then removed.

'Yes, seems good, thanks, but ...' Her lack of confidence was palpable.

'We'll soon see.' The lamp, a bright cyclopic eye, was brought even closer to Skeeter's face.

The Perspex visor and the blue, lower face covering obscured the human features from the person above her. The further lowering of the lamp and the brightness of the light filled Skeeter's vision. She concentrated on the rainbow patterns within the lens as she opened her mouth. For someone who believed little frightened her, this close proximity brought an increased flutter of nerves; it was not the prospect of pain but more the sudden sensory infusion of sounds, tastes and smells, many of which were direct conduits to her childhood phobias.

The dental nurse followed the dentist's actions, guiding the tube to remove excess saliva, the sensation proving a distraction.

'You'll be pleased to know you just need the usual scale and polish. Everything looks fine.' The dentist's hands moved to check her neck and throat. 'You can relax now and have a rinse.'

The chair moved back to upright.

On returning to reception, she booked her next appointment and left. Closing the door, she breathed in the fresh air that slapped her warm face. Her tongue found the new sharp boundaries that now demarcated each tooth; she knew she would find herself doing this until the novelty wore off. *That's it for another six months*, she thought as she slipped the appointment card into her back pocket. As she did so, her phone, still on mute, vibrated. She paused, momentarily closing her eyes. *Why did she know the identity of the caller before she looked at the screen?*

DC Tony Price's voice sounded eager. 'Attempted murder after a botched robbery. Bloody shoplifting in spectacular fashion. Six teenagers from what we can gather, all on three electric motorbikes.'

'What happened to good morning?' She immediately recognised Tony's voice.

'Is it? I wouldn't know. Some of us have our heads to the grindstone.'

'Nose, Tony, it's nose to the grindstone.'

'Whatever, yes, and good morning, if you say so. Anyway, the attack happened ten minutes after the store had opened. Six teenagers, one of these bloody so-called kamikaze raids. All very gung-ho and I guess to them, a challenge and a bit of a laugh. Like tombstoning.' He paused and then continued. 'Not all that innocent, as we have learned that at least one was armed. As in the previous robberies, all were dressed in black, apart from the blood red hoods. Witnesses again suggest the masks had two faces displayed, one on the front and one on the back. Difficult to know if they were coming or bloody going.'

'Janus characters or were they more like Little Red Riding Hood? The world's full of them and they're not all baddies, but there are many with two faces who walk amongst us and breathe the same air. We've all met them, at some time or other,' Skeeter mumbled as she walked down College Road towards her cottage in Roby Mill. She held her phone horizontally in front of her mouth.

'Bloody funny! April said the same. We await CCTV from the store. They buggered off on those electric motorbikes, all in different directions, at some speed, too.'

'You said attempted murder.'

'A shop assistant tried to stop one. Foolish bravery. He pulled at the guy's head covering and received a serious wound to the chest for his trouble. Interestingly, the mask seemed to be attached to the clothing and couldn't be removed.'

'What were they taking?' Skeeter started to jog.

'Anything they could get their thieving hands on but predominantly, mobile phones. This case wouldn't have been assigned to us other than for the excessive violence involved. Our chief believes it's a fledgling gang beginning to flex its muscles. I know you're not in until tomorrow, but I thought you'd want to be involved—'

'Appointment with the tooth fairy today, Tony. Making sure the pearly whites are just that. You should give it a go. The dentist could try to give your smile that ring of confidence but then again, they don't work miracles. I'm sure they could bring a glimmer of hope to that usual grimace of yours.'

'Bloody funny, Wicca. I don't think.'

Skeeter had carried her nickname 'Wicca' from an early age, and it had remained with her throughout her time in the force.

She had been known to some – especially those in the wrestling club – as 'Witch' owing to her name, Warlock, but generally she was Wicca, the derivative of the word witch. It amused Skeeter as they failed to realise that Wicca was the masculine term, that of a sorcerer and not the female version. It was a small consolation.

CHAPTER 6

Skeeter turned off the road and went down the path to her cottage. Tony could hear her heavy breathing as she continued the conversation.

'Must fly, Tony. Remember it's my day off. A day to run, relax and forget about the troubles of work. Lovely day it is to be out of the office.'

Tony groaned. 'You need to train more. Sound totally out of puff. No bloody rest for the wicked, Wicca. Just thought you'd want to know. Sorry for bothering you during your dental beautification.' He hung up and quickly turned his phone round, holding it at face height, before flicking on the camera. Contorting his open mouth into a rictus grin, he tried to inspect his teeth. He then adjusted his head to catch the best light. He failed to see DC Lucy Teraoka move to his side.

'Impressing a lady friend with your charming *risus sardonicus*, Tony?'

He moved the phone, and his face flushed. 'Ya what?'

'*Risus sardonicus*? To you, my detective friend, that's a facial spasm that can be brought on by many things, strychnine poisoning being one of them. Wondered if you'd been chewing your nails.'

Tony pulled the face again. 'What is it with you people? Just been talking to Wicca. She can be a right sarcastic cow and now you ...' Frowning he turned to face her. 'How do my teeth look to you?' The words delivered through stretched lips. Lucy moved closer, tilting her head from side to side.

'How creative do you want me to be?' She did not give him time to answer. 'Predominantly yellow, might be classed as primrose with fine borders and accents of brown. There's a gap to the left and a gold crown down to the right.' She squinted, moving closer. 'There's a number of scabby fillings, too. Not pretty. Happy?'

Tony frowned again. He rubbed a finger across his two front teeth.

'As a matter of interest, when was the last time you saw a dentist or hygienist?' Lucy perched on the edge of his desk.

Tony raised his eyebrows, putting a finger to his lips as if in deep thought. 'Let's say, Lucy, it's been a while.'

'They're too busy chewing what's left of your nails. Try your smile on April. She would like to see you. Just asked me to find you.' She grinned. 'Good luck!'

'Joy of bloody joys.'

Tony moved his chair back. His new office space was luxurious in comparison to the room they had shared at Copy Lane. The space, size and order of the building lent a more positive attitude, a freshness and a modern ambience. Approaching DI April Decent's room, he noted the floor-to-ceiling glazed panels that segregated her personal space were now opaque, as if frosted by a coat of grey. He knocked on the door, took a deep breath and entered. April was staring at an interactive screen on the wall behind one of the desks. The circular LED light that looked like a giant suspended halo, one of many and a design feature of the fifty million pound building, had been turned off allowing a clearer view of the screen.

'Close the door, Tony,' April announced without turning. The fact she had used his first name brought relief. He felt himself relax.

'Lucy said you—'

'We have some CCTV footage of the robbery that took place this morning. I've split the screen to give a better understanding of the sequence of actions. They're in order, pre-, during and post attack.' She tapped the screen, and the first video started. 'The perps appear to have arrived from two directions. The bikes came from both sides of the shop doors. We know the doors on this particular store are always left open.'

Tony moved closer and watched as the pillion passengers leapt from the moving motorbikes. 'They're silent. Scared the living daylights out of those pedestrians.'

'Watch the tall person on the right.' April pointed with a drumstick. 'Tell me, what do you notice?'

'He's wearing a peaked cap and a face covering – surgical, medicinal – like the ones we used during the pandemic.'

April nodded. She paused the video. 'Pedestrian? Member of the public, would you agree?'

Tony allowed his finger to move to his nostril and then he thought better of going further. 'Looks that way but …' He frowned.

'Go on,' April encouraged, arms now folded

'The other pedestrians have all responded to the actions of the black-clad scrotes.' It was a term he regularly used to define perpetrators, irrespective of the company in which he found himself. 'They've clearly panicked.' He pointed to one. 'This one staggered and the lady with him stumbled in her attempt to escape. Many show clear signs of surprise or shock. He, your man, was the only person who appears to remain calm as if it were expected.'

April smiled and raised an eyebrow. 'Watch the next video, it's taken from the internal CCTV cameras. It's a montage as the footage is from different angles to get the best perspective.'

Tony watched what could only be described as a free-for-all as the black-clad figures, black apart from the distinctive, deep red head coverings, seemed to move confidently to their chosen targets. Although there were few shoppers within the store, those there either moved away from the perpetrators as quickly as possible or just stood and watched. Tony saw one customer remove their mobile only to have it immediately snatched. It was at that point he saw the staff member run at the black-clad figure who was standing on one of the display stands kicking off the phones. Within seconds, the member of staff was hanging on to a leg and succeeded in knocking the black-clad figure off balance, pulling him to the ground before attempting to remove the robber's hood. Tony watched as what appeared to be a metal rod was swiftly removed from a sheath attached to the chest area of the masked figure and thrust forcibly a number of times towards the employee, making him release his grip before collapsing holding his chest. 'Bloody hell, he meant that.' Tony leaned closer to the screen. 'That wasn't a knife, was it?' He turned towards April seeking a response.

'Not too sure at this stage, Tony. The staff had been instructed not to attempt to tackle shoplifters, what with knife crime as it is.' She paused the video and started the first recording again. 'We'll know more once the medical report is in. Initial prognosis suggests the injury is not life threatening, I'm pleased to say.' She pointed to a third video, again taken outside during the robbery. 'You see most, if not all of the people outside have moved away, that is apart from three. Two are using their phones to record the incident but the third, the one person with the cap and face covering, is now facing the window. It's what he does next that fascinates me.'

Tony watched as the man moved what looked like a phone to his mouth as he rotated towards the roadside. The man turned his head and looked in both directions. He waved his free hand before moving back towards the window. Within seconds, the black bikes appeared like flocking ravens, silent and stealthy. One drove through the store's open doors whilst the other two perched to either side, like macabre gate guardians. Moments later, the bikes' passengers left the store, tossed bags over their shoulders, mounted and shot off. The man in the cap pocketed his phone and walked away.

'We've picked him up again moments later on camera.' April started the next video, but it was only brief. 'After that, we've nothing. He or she has either gone to ground or got into a car.'

April moved towards the glazed wall and tapped a button. Within seconds the opacity of the glass had cleared. 'I still can't get my head around the technology built into this place.' She chuckled, popping the drumstick next to the other on her desk.

'Why do I have the feeling these robberies are merely trials, tests to develop skills in timing, co-ordination and courage?' It was a rhetorical question, and she did not look at Tony.

'Why? Is my question. What did they get? Mobile phones, laptops and electronic tablets that are worth bugger all in the grand scheme of things, especially considering the trouble that was obviously taken. However, the process worked. If you get away with it once ... I remember my grandad telling me about the docks in the old days. Dockers were called "Desels".' He looked at April and watched her frown. He added a thick Scouse accent. '"Dese'll do for de wife and dese'll do for Ma and Pa."

They'd try to nick anything that they could and walk out through the dock gates; Tinned stuff, salmon, whatever was available that could be stuck up your coat.'

April laughed and sat down as Tony continued.

'The docks were really busy then and the police used plain-clothes lads to patrol, always in twos. The dockers referred to the mobile dock section of the police as magpies because, like the birds, they were considered a bloody nuisance.'

April leaned back fascinated as his tale unfolded. 'You're a mine of information, Tony.'

'Useless, my mother would say.' He grinned and wondered if he should ask April to give her opinion on his teeth but then thought better of it.

'In those days it was clearly an expected practice that lacked structure. These "Desels", however,' she pointed to the empty screen behind, 'are a different kettle of fish. They're not nicking for their ma or pa. They are, as you put it so well, probably honing skills or stealing to order. Maybe it's a newly formed gang or part of—'

April's desk phone rang. 'DI Decent.' She listened. 'He is lucky indeed.' As she responded she kept glancing at Tony. 'Have you sent the full report? Thanks, I appreciate your swift response on this.'

Tony leaned on the opposite chair. Even though the building was state of the art, old habits were clearly evident in the arrangement of the office furniture.

'A metal kitchen knife sharpener, steel, most kitchens have one, ground to a point, it was the weapon used. Not dissimilar to the old sword stick. Easily concealed and very effective as a thrusting weapon.'

'Also, it would provide a good defence against a blade or fist.' Tony demonstrated by pretending to hold the weapon and moving it with sweeping motions diagonally across his body.

'The bikes have been used for solitary phone and bag snatches for a few years now but this, and a couple of previous focused robberies, appear to be more specific, more ordered. Something, Tony, is brewing.'

CHAPTER 7

Caitlin Byrne's two friends huddled round her phone, their facial expressions constantly changing. They were oblivious to the background chatter. The pub was busy for the early evening, but they had found a reasonably quiet corner.

'Bloody hell, hun, I'd have been out of there as quick as.' Holding the phone, Stephanie squealed, her excitement clear. She stretched out a hand and placed it on Caitlin's. 'Proper little soldier you are.'

'It scared me, but I just had to catch it. You see them posted all the time, London, Rome but actually to be involved here. I couldn't believe it was happening. I posted it immediately on my socials and had a brilliant response. Mind, I've also had the usual knobheads. I've never seen anything like it for real before. It was all over quick like. In and out in a flash.'

'Why does it make me think of my Mark on a Saturday night?' Steph pulled a face and the three burst into fits of laughter. A number of the other customers in the bar turned to look.

'I heard about it on the news. Not you and Mark.' The giggles began again. 'They had some CCTV stuff. A close-up, too, of the strange mask things they were wearing,' Jan added. 'You can see them on Caitlin's video. Pause it, Steph ... no it's gone past. Give it here!' Jan snatched the phone, and her fingers played on the screen. 'There, see that?' She held the phone to face each in turn. It was then paused again. 'Bloody hell, he looks totally cringe-worthy, the one in the cap and the mask. He's looking directly at you, hun.'

Caitlin took the phone and with her fingers, enlarged the image. 'Do you know, I never noticed him, and I've looked at this loads of times. I don't think he was one of them.'

'You may well be right. He's only seen towards the end when the robbin' bastards make a dash for it,' Jan said reassuringly, spotting the look of uncertainty on Steph's face. 'Probably oblivious, more than likely pissed or on drugs but still spots our Caitlin's beauty in all of the chaos.'

'Thanks very much you cheeky minx, some compliment that is. Anyway, it's your round, Steph, unless you suddenly need to go for a wee?' The laughter erupted again. It was going to be one of those evenings.

* * *

Within hours, Caitlin was the worse for wear; the double gins had left their mark. The girls all got into an Uber and made sure she was safe in her flat before they returned to the waiting car.

'Fuck, Jan. She's well lit. Did you see if anyone spiked her drink?'

Jan shook her head. 'She'd started before we came out, I bet. She only had what we had. I'll check with her in the morning.'

CHAPTER 8

The dashboard clock showed 08.33 as Skeeter drove past Copy Lane, her old police base, as she headed towards Netherton and then the docks at Crosby. Copy Lane was still operational as a holding station but most of the key staff had been moved either to Rose Hill or the Operational Command Centre at Speke. This was not Skeeter's normal route, but she needed to stop in the centre of Liverpool. She had pre-arranged a late start to her shift, it should give her enough time. She needed a new phone as her old one had not taken kindly to falling from her back pocket into the toilet while she had been inspecting her teeth in the bathroom mirror the previous evening. Allowing it to sit in a box of rice had made no difference, no matter how confident the internet article had been.

After parking in the underground at Liverpool One shopping centre, she made her way to the upper level on South St John Street. Glancing at her watch, she saw it was now just after nine. The Apple store opened at 9.30. To kill time, she decided to take a quick look at the old Merseyside Police Headquarters, a few minutes' walk away. She paused at Custom House Place and looked across the bus station towards the familiar red brick building. The copper-coloured windows within the eight floors always brought a smile to her face. *What other colour could they be?* She mused. Now, however, the building was to be sold, it was prime real estate in the centre of the city and like Copy Lane, the coppers had moved to the recently commissioned new stations.

Turning to go back, she was startled as two electric motorbikes raced through the bus station heading in the opposite direction to the traffic before turning onto the pedestrian area. The riders, both dressed in black, gave little heed to the shoppers. It was the speed and the lack of noise that struck Skeeter, they were like swift moving shadows, manoeuvrable and stealthy. Her mind went to the conversation she had shared with Tony the previous day.

'There's never a copper around when you need one unless someone hears you say hurty bloody words,' an elderly woman grumbled loudly as she looked directly at Skeeter. 'Getting to be a right bloody nuisance what with electric scooters and bikes available to all and sundry by this useless council. Two thousand of the bloody things they've got. They leave them anywhere without a thought for others, you know. That's the bloody trouble today. People have no respect. Wasn't like that when I was your age, I can tell you. They need to be paying more to us pensioners and bringing back the winter fuel allowance rather than squandering money on them stupid contraptions.'

She turned and made her way towards a waiting bus, still grumbling. Skeeter had said nothing but, without a doubt, she agreed with much of what she had said.

* * *

Caitlin Byrne stepped off the bus, she was late as usual. The throbbing in her head did nothing for her mood. Pushing the door, she dashed into Blakey's restaurant. Hugo was wiping down the bar. He turned to the huge clock above the bottle-lined shelves and then back at Caitlin, an action that was totally deliberate.

'A bit early for night school. What time do you call this, like?' He folded his arms. His English was clearly his second language, even though the vowels were flat. He had been in Liverpool a number of years.

'Sorry, the alarm didn't go off and the bus was delayed in traffic. Accident on Oxford Street, too. It would have been quicker to walk from there but with the rain starting, you know how it is. Give us a water, Hugo, my mouth is like the bottom of a budgie's cage.'

Filling a glass, he put it on the counter. 'We start service in ten minutes. Amanda and I have done what you should have been doing an hour or so ago. It'll come off your wages.'

She drank the water. 'Shit! Really? You're kidding, right?' She giggled as if he were joking.

Hugo raised an eyebrow and turned his head at an angle. His expression suggested the answer she did not want. 'If you don't like it, don't take off your coat. Go home and let the budgie back into the cage!' He paused but the quip fell on stony ground. 'We'll continue to manage without you. I can sort out what we owe you by the end of the day. You can then stay in bed as long as you like. We can cope. After all, we have done so far today. This is a business, my business, not a bloody charity and it runs by having a committed and dedicated staff.'

'I've said I'm sorry.' Caitlin started to remove her coat.

'Like you said the time before and the time before that. I've had a change of heart ...' He paused and a smile prematurely rushed to Caitlin's lips. 'No, it's not working. In my country to be punctual is also to be respectful and polite. I've changed my mind.' He looked directly at her. 'I've just terminated your employment as from Tuesday, when you last worked, as it was your day off yesterday. Now leave. We'll find someone who's committed and can get in on time.'

There was a silence as Caitlin looked first at Hugo and then Amanda. Amanda turned away, out of embarrassment and went into the kitchen. Hugo pointed to the door.

'We're not in your fucking country, we're in mine. We always said you were an arrogant twat of a boss, full of your own foreign self-importance. I'll expect my wages as soon as … and don't forget my share of the tips. Prick!' She thrust her middle finger in Hugo's direction, collected her bag and left. The confident departure was pure bravado as inside she was crumbling, realising her bridge had truly been burned.

The rain was now stronger, the noise of the traffic on wet roads seemed to dominate. She was crying, the weather mirroring her feelings. She needed a drink. Turning onto Dale Street, the rain seemed lighter but blew in veils, fine as mist but uncomfortably wet. The sky brought a silvery sheen to the road. Looking past the town hall, she saw the clock on the Liver Building: 11.47. She sighed. The look she had received from Hugo was still clear, as were her words, which she now regretted. She felt like shedding more tears.

The pub offered a welcome relief; she spotted a seat in the far corner. It was busier than she had expected. She was shortly followed through the door by a man shaking his umbrella. Collecting a gin and tonic she moved to the seat, taking out her phone.

'Hi Caitlin. I can't chat, I'm working.' There was silence. 'Caitlin, you okay, hun?' There was clear concern in Stephanie's voice at Caitlin's sobbing.

'That shit of a boss, Hugo, has sacked me. I got in late.'

'Bloody hell. I warned you last time. It's work, they expect you to be there on time.'

'There's roadworks at the roundabout near the end of my road, something to do with gas. We were diverted round the houses. Nineteen minutes it should take the 52 bus to get to Queen Square. I could have walked it quicker with a nail in my clog.'

One person at the bar moved, looked and then turned away.

'Did Jan ring you this morning?'

'Yes, I had a missed call at just after seven. I didn't hear it. Didn't hear the fucking alarm, neither. What with that and the bus …'

'Did you have much before we went out last night?'

'Sorry, I should have said, thanks for seeing me home. I don't know what came over me. Yes, I had a couple of scoops. Small ones.' Caitlin, for the first time, giggled. 'You know me, babe.'

* * *

Driving down Leeward Drive, Skeeter turned onto the one-way entry to the Police Operational and Command Centre before bumping over the sleeping policeman. For some reason it always made her think of Tony. She approached the security gates. Irrespective of visual identification, Skeeter handed over her ID to be scanned. A look back at the car for further confirmation and then back at the screen was executed before the ID was returned and the gate opened. Within minutes, she would be parked.

Slipping the lanyard round her neck she passed through further security before taking the stairs to her department. It was a far cry from Copy Lane. She tossed her bag onto her desk and glanced at her colleagues.

'This room's like an airport lounge to me. Still can't get over it.'

As if on cue, a paper aircraft, triangular with a pointed nose, flew a circuitous route before crashing into the desk divider, coming to rest a short distance from her feet. She knew from where it had taken off. Picking it up she unfolded the origami plane and read what was written. 'Afternoon. Your turn to make a brew.' Tony's head popped up from some distance away.

'Coffee with one would be great, ta!'

'You should talk to Peter to see if there are any vacancies in the drone team. With skills like yours, I'm sure you'd be in with a chance.' Skeeter scrunched the note into a ball and tossed it into the bin.

'You and Pete still a couple? "Fly me to the moon ..."' He sang.

'Behave,' Skeeter warned, pointing her finger in his direction.

'They've got seven operators. A full squadron as far as I'm aware, Wicca. I heard your fella was on a week's training.' Tony stood and leaned on one of the dividers.

'He's in Leeds. Flying a new style drone. Over thirty grand's worth as far as I know. All bells and whistles.'

Tony whistled. She looked at him to see if he was taking the proverbial. 'The secret eye in the sky. They're so versatile now. They're even changing the face of war.'

Moving through the open-planned office she saw April chatting with DC Kasum Kapoor. Popping her head round the door she nodded. Thrusting a thumb in the air. 'Personal communication equipment is back up and running.' She waved her new phone.

April smiled. 'Need to see you in ten.'

* * *

Caitlin ran her finger round the empty glass. Her main worry was how to pay the bills, she needed to find work quickly.

'You all right, love?' The heavy Scouse accent startled her. It was so strong that it sounded fake. The man who had followed her in, stood before her resting both hands on his clumsily wrapped umbrella. 'Didn't want to intrude but … well, I saw you on the phone and then wipe away a tear. A problem shared is a problem halved, as my old mam used to say or something like that.' He smiled. 'Maybe I could just get you another drink?'

Caitlin chuckled, not the most original chat-up line she had heard. She shook her head and sighed, more out of her own frustration than anything else. 'Thanks, but no. I now have a lot to do.' Standing she collected her phone and put it in her bag before slipping out from behind the table.

'Another time, maybe. Sorry to have disturbed you only I …' He deliberately left the sentence hanging. 'Haven't we met before?'

Caitlin looked at her shoes. He was nothing if not persistent. 'I don't think so.' She altered her gaze and looked him directly in the eye to make sure he understood she was neither in the mood for games nor feeling amicable. She noted his tie, trying to think of the last man she had seen in a pub wearing one. She turned swiftly, before he could speak.

Out of the pub, she was pleased to see the rain had stopped and the roads were drying where the car wheels ran. Within minutes, she was walking down Victoria Street. She was being followed. The buildings on either side were both grand in size and architectural style, not that either aesthetic was of any interest to her. Many held restaurants and bars, and she glanced at the windows optimistically. Just by the Lisbon Building she saw a 'staff wanted' note in the window of an Irish bar. Her heart fluttered. She entered.

Unbeknown to her, she was being watched. Tucking the umbrella beneath his arm, the man googled bus route 52. He followed the route shown on the map before calling a taxi. He needed to get to his car.

* * *

The barman held the glass, checking it against the light before giving it a further rub with a cloth.

'Caitlin, you said your name was? You have waited on before?'

Answering in the affirmative to each of the questions, she felt optimistic.

'Leave me your number. If you have the experience that you say you have, I'll call you later. If all goes well, Caitlin, you say you could start on a trial basis tomorrow?'

She nodded. A broad smile creased her face. 'I could, yes.'

'We'll discuss hourly rate and stuff should I call. Do you have references?' Her face fell.

'I got in late for my last job a couple of times and … well … I'll understand if you don't call but I've learned a valuable lesson.'

He laughed. 'We've all made mistakes.' He winked. 'But then as you so rightly say, we hopefully learn from them. It would be on a trial basis. You understand that?'

'Indeed. I was foolish. Thank you.' She took a deep breath.

Having left her number, she came out of the bar onto the roadside. Her despair had quickly turned to an excited nervousness. *Let's hope he calls,* she thought as she crossed the road and wandered down Stanley Street, for no other reason than she lived on a Stanley Road and was curious. She immediately wondered who Stanley might have been to have so many streets, roads and a park named after him. Dr Livingstone came to mind, but she could not recall the link. If she remembered, she would look it up on her way home. To her left was the statue of Eleanor Rigby, a rough bronze of a forlorn female. *'All the lonely people,'* she sang in a whisper. 'Don't let yourself turn into one of those, do you hear?' She continued but nobody heard. The image of the stranger she had met in the pub flashed in her mind. 'You don't have problems pulling fellas, girl, it's just a case of finding the right one.'

* * *

The bus ride home was without incident and the fictitious roadworks had magically disappeared; so, too, had her desire to discover who Stanley was. Leaving the bus, she crossed the road and paused momentarily at Kings Gardens. It was a green oasis in a busy area, but it was a mere shadow of what it once might have been. In recent months, it had witnessed more than its fair share of antisocial behaviour, including stabbings. The police had fought to cleanse the area by having a greater presence and yet it had become a no-go zone after dark for many. *I go from a King to a Queen daily on the 52 bus*, she mused knowing nothing could be further from the truth. Her one-bed flat was just further down Stanley Road. Reaching her flat, she saw that a discarded pizza box had blown into the entrance and lodged against the outer door. She swiftly moved it with her foot until it was on the pavement.

The area never seemed to change. Many of the shops located on the street comprised either take aways, general stores or were shuttered. However, a couple of barber shops had opened recently, their neon lights adding a degree of vivid flashing colour to what were best described as drab façades. Pausing, Caitlin wondered how they could be viable, positioned so closely together. She had heard rumours they might not be what they seemed.

Before she could remove her coat, her phone rang.

'Caitlin, it's Cillian, you called in earlier, the Irish bar. You can still start tomorrow, yes?'

'Cillian, how Irish are we? Yes, that's lovely news, ta.'

'Indeed. I liked your name and your honesty. That would be

perfect. Start at 10. Don't be late. We'll discuss the finer details tomorrow.'

'I'll be there.' The excitement bubbled in her response.

Delighted with the news, she immediately called Steph. She checked her watch. It was just after four thirty.

'I've got a new job. Long story. As you know that shit of a human, Hugo, gave me the bum's rush for being late but I've managed to find a new one, I start tomorrow. How clever am I? I also got chatted up, so there must be some life in this *petit visage* still.' She chuckled. 'Listen, just nipping to get a bottle to celebrate. Give me a ring in about twenty minutes or pop round early evening if you can but I'm having an early night.'

'Suddenly, everything's early with you, Caitlin Byrne.'

'I've seen the light,' She giggled. 'I needed a job, and I needed it badly.'

'Well done! Remember it is a job and not a game. Don't spoil it with the booze. I'll try and pop round. It could be about half seven. Chat soon.' Steph hung up.

CHAPTER 9

April straightened some paperwork as she gestured Skeeter towards a chair. 'Tony says you're aware of the physical attack that took place during the robbery. There's clear evidence to suggest it's the same gang from two of four similar previous robberies. However, this is the first where a serious weapon has been used and therefore it's fallen into our in-tray. We have a DNA sample taken from the fingernail swab collected from the employee who attempted to stop one of them but as yet, nothing's coming up on the national database. We've also checked CCTV footage from the previous sites. Interestingly, Skeeter, we have a common denominator and that's a member of the public.' She arranged three photographs on her desk in chronological order. 'We actually have two if you count the bizarre hoods.'

Skeeter came around the table. 'Male or female?'

'Unsure. However, we have an approximate height, five eleven and according to the people who know these things, weighing about seventy-five kilograms.'

Skeeter looked directly at April. 'If you ask me for a guess, then I'd say male.'

Returning Skeeter's eye contact was never easy, she suffered from heterochromia iridium. Having one startling blue eye and one very dark brown gave the appearance there was no pupil, making the eye not too dissimilar to a black void, causing the onlooker to focus on the blue.

April nodded. 'The person is sporting different headgear in each photograph taken from images captured from CCTV footage and yet they are always wearing a face covering. Strange how the pandemic gave rise to youths using them to hide their identity and now there's nothing we can do about it. They also wear hoodies, leaving the least facial area visible. Pop on a pair of sunglasses and you kill any chance of facial recognition.'

Skeeter scoffed, knowing too well the difficulties experienced by the latest street wear. 'Every orchestra needs a conductor. This character looks to be a watchman, an overseer. Anything gleaned from the others involved?'

April laughed. 'They're dressed like shadows, nothing distinctive and yet the red head coverings are all slightly different, not in each attack, but for each individual. We've enlarged some of the clearer images.'

Moving to the interactive board she found the file. Both looked at the enlarged photographs. 'To me, Skeeter, the facial features seem to be sewn, a kind of patchwork, a fabric collage. Coloured material has been roughly sewn to the hood to form the irregular facial features. The broad, thick stitching around the shapes and to the edges of the torn holes for eyes and mouth have probably been created to look like menacing sutures. It's also reminiscent of some kind of uniform, if that's not a contradiction.'

'There were a few professional wrestlers, not my style of wrestling, more the entertaining type, WWE, who wore hoods.' Skeeter rubbed her eyes. 'It's the dual faces, back and front that makes them so original.'

'There's a lot of work in each one making them quite individual. The hood is attached to the upper clothing, too, probably for security. On one of the attacks,' April quickly referenced the date and place, 'they had just the one stitched face. In the latest, they had a face to the back as well as the front. They're very individual … identifiable, in fact. The differentiation is possibly clear only to those in the gang and the overseer, making them manageable and therefore accountable.'

The expression on Skeeter's face suggested she had not considered that possibility. 'Indeed. Sorry but I've paperwork to complete for the drug bust we did yesterday. How many more homes and buildings have been turned into domestic cannabis farms in this fair city of ours? I'll go through all the facts of this when that's done.' Skeeter openly smiled, hoping the latest cosmetic dentistry would be noticed. She was rather too optimistic.

'Thanks. Liaise with Tony on this, will you. It could get worse before …' She prematurely ended her own sentence with one raised eyebrow.

* * *

Caitlin propped open the front door to the flat with the fire extinguisher that had parted company with the wall long before she had rented the flat, having left a small but gaping hole. She checked the road and ran across to the general store. The shop seemed empty; music drifted down each aisle. She paused momentarily, trying to identify the song, before collecting a tube of Pringles. The alcohol was displayed along with cigarettes and vapes behind a grubby Perspex screen, all segregated from the rest of the shop. It was within the shopkeeper's secure domain; anything of value remained out of reach. The large screen showing multiple images from various CCTV cameras was clear for her to see. She requested a bottle of white wine with a screw top, the quality and price had no bearing on her choice. She paid by card.

'Have a good evening, love.' The shopkeeper's accent, clearly not local, had a musical lilt; ending with the word 'love', it had a familiar ring.

She smiled and left, crossing the road. Tucking the Pringles and the wine beneath her arm, she moved the extinguisher, kicking closed the main entrance door to the flats before mounting the uncarpeted flight of stairs. Her footsteps echoed in the confines of the hallway as she arrived at her flat door – that, too, had not been locked. From being totally despondent earlier in the day, she now felt a new feeling of elation, as if the dark clouds had parted to reveal an optimistic silver lining. The tune to 'Mr Blue Sky' popped into her head. She stared at the room. The living space was a kitchen and lounge area. If her failings for alcohol and lack of punctuality were weaknesses, her ability to keep an orderly home was a strength. Even though it was small, it was clean and immaculate, some might also say minimalist. She had good neighbours, who were discreet and supportive. The elderly couple above had been friendly and understanding since she had moved in.

After hanging up her coat, she moved to the cupboard, collected a bowl for the crisps and a wine glass before pouring herself a glass. She flopped onto the settee, kicked off her shoes and put her feet on the coffee table. 'May these be the worst of our days,' she said out loud, raising the glass. 'To the Irish.' Her thoughts flashed to Cillian, and she felt a flutter in her tummy as a smile swiftly spread. 'You can stop that, girl,' she reprimanded herself whilst trying to control her giggles. She took another sip.

'I'll have a couple of drinks, watch some television and then have an early night.' She spoke out loud. She giggled as she realised that she was talking to herself. She had just settled when her phone rang. It was neither on the table nor the settee and yet it seemed close by. The ringing stopped the moment it landed on the settee next to her. She squealed, startled by the sudden motion, the wine sloshed from the glass onto her lap.

* * *

Steph stood gazing at the television, her phone to her ear. Caitlin's phone had rung to start with but now seemed to be dead. She tried twice more but again, no response. She would wait thirty minutes and call again. Failing that, she would go round.

* * *

Even though it was late, Tony checked his computer again. The request had been worth sending. He printed the results and crossed the room to Skeeter's desk. He did not wait for her to look up.

'Remember the people on the video who didn't panic but used their phones to capture the robbery?'

'No, but do go on.' Skeeter rested her chin on her hands.

'Well, digital forensics have tracked down one of them who posted the footage on her social media platforms. Apparently, tracing them was relatively easy. Anyway, we now have a name. Caitlin Byrne. They're checking for further contact details. She could have further footage or be better able to describe the man we now believe to be involved. I've left a lead for Michael to chase when he gets it.'

'*The Conductor*? Good. Keep me posted as soon as you hear anything.'

He checked his watch. 'Will do but that'll be tomorrow, then. It's home time.'

* * *

Caitlin was transfixed on the bizarre face that stared back. A gasp of a squeal erupted from her lips. The scalene features on the hood were disconcerting and frightening. She shifted her stiffening body across the settee in a feeble and yet futile effort to put distance between them. She felt herself urinate uncontrollably.

'Make another sound and it will, I assure you, be your last.' The words were delivered soft, contradictory to their meaning. However, in another way, the softness reinforced the threat. She could discern no real accent. The speech was measured, the words ending deliberately and accurately, none was clipped or rushed, as if time was of no consequence. But her understanding of each and every word was of vital importance.

Caitlin's eyes remained fixed to the figure's red hood. The embarrassment of the dampness between her thighs had receded as a greater fear came into focus. The contrasting patchwork of random, coloured geometric shapes created a face made up of asymmetrical eyes, nose and mouth, which were not only disconcerting but eerily disturbing, reminding her immediately of the robbery she had witnessed. Her mouth moved to protest but no sound and no words were emitted. They remained trapped, stifled somewhere in her throat. All that came out was a gurgle of involuntary breath accompanied by copious saliva down her chin.

'We have met before, even though we have not been formally introduced. In the pub, you mentioned bus 52, nineteen minutes, remember?' He spoke deliberately with little hesitation.

Her ashen face still showed no signs of comprehension.

'No? I thought not. Strange, but I also knew you before that. I am familiar with you as @RealCat, or that is the name under which you post on your socials. I've seen your photographs, those of your friends, too … Steph? She is a friend, yes? You have many so-called friends.'

Caitlin frowned, trying to make sense of what she was seeing and hearing.

'And although I've looked through many of your social media posts since you kindly accepted my friend request, many do not interest me, yet there is one that does, one that upset me greatly, more than you could ever comprehend.' He saw her glance at the door. 'You would be dead before you left this settee. Trust me, but you can try if you wish. God loves a trier, but the Devil always takes his chance.'

Caitlin contorted her face, more out of confusion than understanding.

'Looking at your posts, I note you enjoy making videos.' He paused in recognition as she nodded. 'And yet you don't under-stand, do you?' His hand pointed to his hood. 'Does this not give you the smallest of clues?'

Her head moved from side to side and then up and down as if controlled by invisible strings.

'You can speak, just don't scream or shout, @RealCat.'

'The robbery?' Her voice was weak and shaky.

'Clever girl. In one. Why did you post it? Now that's the real question. Do you know what harm interfering members of the public like you do to people?'

She shook her head.

'No, I didn't think so. There's just too many of you. Why didn't you help the others, the lady who fell for one? Why did you not ring the police? Why didn't you do something positive? All too often the phone comes out and the camera goes on like an intrusive, watchful eye. We see it all of the time when people have accidents, fights in pubs, even when people are in distress. The majority of those close enough to help and assist don't. What do they do? Like you, they take out their phones and film as if abrogating all human responsibility to one's fellow man. My question to you, Cat. May I call you, Cat?'

She nodded again.

'My question is why?' He came and sat next to her on the settee. 'You know I could kill you here and now. It would take but one swift action. I have that skill. Now here's a question for you to consider. Let's imagine that in the next few moments I were to do just that, kill you here in your flat. Would you like me to film it? Film your final moments and then post it on your socials? Imagine if there were someone else here, Caitlin, would you want them to help you or film your demise?'

Caitlin's face contorted, trying to comprehend the incomprehensible. 'To help me.' She stuttered before starting to cry, a sudden flush of tears that ran in one continuous flow as her guttural gasps returned.

'I thought so as those images, those cruel and evil captured moments, would be there forever. Your suffering wouldn't evaporate or vanish as it would be held, digitally trapped, forever and indelible for the curious, the scrolling masses eager for a cheap thrill. Yes, Caitlin, for ever. Some viewers might even find it sexually arousing. Can you believe that? I personally find that distasteful. So let me ask you again. Why didn't you help your fellow human beings?'

'I don't know, I'm sorry, I don't. Please. I didn't even think.' She wiped her face with her sleeve, a snail trail of silvery snot coloured the dark material. Her shoulders heaved, rising and falling involuntarily.

'Like the rest of your generation in this world today … you do not think. Did you hope to get some attention from your so-called 'friends', is that it? Or is it more like attracting some kind of fame?' The cynical laughter that followed was muffled behind the hood, but she felt the warmth of the breath permeate the fabric. 'You're pathetic. You need to think, think why I'm here.

Many, many months ago, we would not have been having this conversation, as there was no need then, there was no anger in me. You could never understand how small, possibly insignificant things can change a person. How could you? How could anybody? I could not at first but then the hatred grew like a cancer.' There was an immediate pause. For a moment she thought she heard a whimper, a sniffling as if he were holding back tears. 'No one would understand, no one, so why should a silly girl like you?'

* * *

He lifted his phone pointing the camera at the frightened girl. The screen was filled with Caitlin's face as she looked directly at the back of the phone, the small rings, the lenses, looked like spiders' eyes. He flicked to video and pressed start, they both heard the familiar sound, a ping. She frowned clearly uncertain as to what was now expected of her. Moving the phone into his left hand he slowly focused it higher. As hoped, she lifted her face following the trajectory of the camera exposing her neck and jaw. His straight, driving punch came from low to high, a perfectly executed uppercut. Her body stiffened and twitched as she collapsed sideways and then back. Her hands moved towards her head in unison but stopped at chest height and shook violently for a second or more as her fingers spread wide. Stopping the camera, he reached into his pocket and retrieved a transparent, polythene bag before grabbing her hair with his gloved hand and lifting her head at an angle, allowing the bag to cover it and her neck. A large, black electrician's tie wound round her neck over the bag and was pulled taut, tight enough to sink into her soft flesh and constrict her airway. A light film of condensation quickly blurred the area close to her mouth and nose and the bag gripped the features of her face. He was surprised, after the blow she had received, there appeared to be no blood emanating from either her mouth or nose. Her eyes remained closed. He started the camera on his phone again carefully panning away from the settee. It was done.

He turned the phone off. 'Sorry!' The words were but a whisper, but they were sincere.

Collecting Caitlin's phone, he took her hand. Her finger print opened her phone. He quickly changed the password.

Opening the apartment door, he dropped the latch, removed the keys and closed it locking it from the outside. Removing his hood, he thrust it into his overcoat pocket whilst descending the stairs; he was in no hurry. An aroma of cooking filled his nostrils, it seemed to linger in the emptiness of the hallway. He paused to identify the food, failing before his gloved hand flicked the latch on the outer door. Within minutes, he was passing the parkland on Stanley Road, South Bootle Park. His car was not far away, and by the time he had started the engine, he knew she would be dead. It had proved to be easier than he had imagined. Then again, it had not been his first.

* * *

Stephanie was growing more anxious as she slipped on her coat. She tried to ring Caitlin one more time. The phone was still dead.

CHAPTER 10

Stephanie instinctively kicked the empty pizza box further away as she pressed the button for Flat 2. There was no response. She tried once more, leaving her finger on the button for some time. Nothing. She then pressed the button for Flat 4.

'Hello?' The voice sounded old but assured, the crackle of the intercom did not help.

'Mrs Fellows, it's Steph, Caitlin's friend. Caitlin asked me to call round but she's not answering the door, nor her phone. Have you seen her?'

'Hello, Steph, love. I saw her go out earlier. She crossed the road. Didn't see her come home, but I was watching telly straight after, see, and my Bert's asleep in his chair. He's always asleep these days. Not heard her in the flat either. Do you want me to pop down and check?'

'Please, if it's not too much trouble.'

'Give us a mo', pet.'

Steph stood in the entrance area and focused on the empty pizza box lying to the side before directing her gaze to the row of shops opposite. The day's light was fading and for the first time the sky had definition, a careless colourwash of oranges and reds. The temperature contradicted the perceived warmth.

'Are you still there, love?'

'Yes.'

'I've knocked proper loud but there's no reply, love. Maybe she's still out. You know what she's like. Might have met a new man.' She giggled. 'More likely popped into the pub knowing Cat.'

'Do you have a key to her flat, Mrs Fellows?'

'No, love. She gives us one if she's expecting a delivery, we don't have one permanently.'

'Sorry to trouble you. Thanks. If you see h—' She didn't get chance to finish.

'No trouble. It's what neighbours do. If we see her, we'll tell her you called. Better still, I'll call you when I see her. Give us your number. I'll get a pen, if you'll give us a minute, love.' She seemed to be gone some time. 'You can never find one when you need one and then there's two in the same drawer, like buses really! Ready.'

Steph told her the number then repeated it.

'Night, love.' The crackling of the intercom stopped.

Steph stood on the pavement and looked up towards Caitlin's flat window. There was no light. *I'll bloody well kill her when I see her.* Wrapping her coat around herself, more out of protest than a need for warmth, she left.

* * *

DC Michael Peet was on lates, he was always on lates. He enjoyed the station when it was not operating at full blast, although since moving to the new building, it never seemed to have the same nocturnal lull. Nevertheless, he could still concentrate. He had always intended to be a lawyer but his partner's pregnancy in his second year of university had stopped that idea in its tracks. Quickly married, he joined the force and with the arrival of a second and then a third child, he realised his police career was the one on which he should focus. Working lates also gave him respite from the children. Slipping the lanyard identity tag into his top shirt pocket, he popped his head around April's door.

'Have you got used to living in a glass bowl?' He kept a straight face.

'Better than the previous office, so mustn't grumble, Michael. How are the kids?'

'At home.' He grinned and rubbed his hands together. 'Love 'em really.' He winked.

'Tony wants you to chase up some social sites of a Caitlin Byrne. There's no need to go to town on it as digital forensics have done much of the spade work. He's asked them to create a spurious friend request using a fictitious Facebook page. That's done, and in the system, if you need it. It can be used if you have any worries once you have an overview of the woman. Tony has a suspicion she might have some link with the person we believe was controlling the attack. Maybe they were working together. See what you can find and I'm sure you will use your discretion. This type of action can be a tad sensitive.' Her facial expression suggested that some things had to be done to move an investigation forward. 'Thanks, have a good evening. I have an appointment with a dog.'

* * *

Even though the light was fading, Colin and Sue Martin, the couple who owned the farm and the cottage April rented, were in the yard when she pulled up. Tico, her rescue greyhound, was standing close to Sky, Sue's border collie. Both looked at the car but neither moved.

'Some welcome that is from my own dog.' She threw her bag over her shoulder.

'Don't take it personally, Colin has food in his pocket. Their attention is fixed firmly there. Good day? Fancy a brew, or something stronger?'

'Seeing Tico has relegated me to a second-class citizen that would make me feel most welcome.'

The cottage had been a lucky find when she had moved to Merseyside. Positioned on the coast just north of Liverpool, it was close enough to the city for a short commute but far enough away to feel as though she were surrounded by nature. But it was the coastline that was the real draw, the edge of the land that had convinced her it was the right place. The length of beach and wooded dunes that seemed to go as far as the eye could see, the western sunsets and the call of the gulls, all conspired to make it a perfect home.

The kitchen was warm, and the stove not only produced heat but also a delicious aroma. Sue poured two large glasses of red wine. 'Cheers!' Both glasses touched.

'So, Chef, what's cooking?'

'Hotpot, your dog is about to enjoy the offcuts. I'll be sending over a plate in about an hour if you'd like?' Sue tilted her head and raised an eyebrow, anticipating the answer.

'The day gets better and better. How's his Lordship been?' April asked, referring to Tico.

'If I could sleep for half the amount of time he does ...' Sue shook her head. 'He's so good with Sky, they're best buddies even though they hated each other when you first arrived here. They've both been with Colin most of the afternoon.'

'He'll sleep the clock round if I'd let him.'

April had been concerned about leaving her dog for the

length of time she was working as her hours could be so irregular but, now, she had no worries. He was in good hands.

'Busy fighting crime?' Sue asked as she glanced at the clock on the kitchen wall.

'County line gangs are still extremely active. Using kids to run the drugs, sucking them in with promises of designer goods, phones and the like. Trouble is, they fail to see that their so-called "friendly handler" cares not one jot about them and will happily throw them to the wolves. We often pick up the pieces when you have rival gangs, each putting a toe into the another's area. It's then that things get rough and some even go missing. Calling on their parent with bad news—'

'Parent?' Sue sipped some wine before checking the oven.

'It's amazing how often these kids are from broken homes. Then there's the ever-growing postcode gangs, bringing bitter rivalry, and now knives and machetes are key tools in their armoury ...' April did not need to finish.

Sue shivered. 'We've seen it on the news, it's so depressing. We wonder whether bringing children into this world is the responsible thing to do these days. It was never like this when we were growing up, or maybe we were protected from it. My parents always used to say the summers were hotter, people were kinder ...'

April nodded. 'Mars Bars were bigger.' She giggled as she lifted her wine glass. 'My parents said that, too. You only have to walk on Crosby beach to know that it wasn't always sunshine and roses. For five miles you can walk on the rubble of blitzed Liverpool: masonry of all kinds dumped along the coast after the May 1941 bombings. I don't consider four thousand civilians killed and seventy thousand made homeless a walk in the park.'

'No,' Sue topped up their wine, 'but there was community spirit back then, people looked out for each other, they were all facing the same foe, the same uncertainty. I believe people were kinder and had more time for others and I don't just mean neighbours. I despair at some things you see all the time now. When there's any kind of incident, whether involving a large or small audience, people constantly whip out their phones and video the misfortune of others rather than assist. I know that's a broad statement, but you know what I mean. And, true, come to think of it, Mars Bars were bigger.' They both laughed again.

Colin came in followed by Sky. 'Something funny? The big fella's curled in front of your Aga. He's had enough.'

'Speaking of "enough",' April finished her wine. 'It's time for some mindless creativity, I have a piece of stained glass I should try to bring to fruition. Thank you, you don't know how much I needed this.'

Michael Peet watched the videos of the robbery and then looked at the social media pages for @RealCat before reviewing the created Facebook page for the friend request. He laughed out loud at the tag, @MicKnight. All the elements had been assimilated including profile and image, interests and friends as well as a number of posts. Further reading also confirmed what the forensic technicians had discovered – that her name was Caitlin Byrne. From there it was easy for Michael to find many of her personal details including an address. As he did so, the tech people's comment flooded his consciousness: *once you have one key piece, it can unlock a web of information.* Through records held, he was quickly able to find her place of work and also discover her police record, of which there were two listed offences, both for being drunk and disorderly. In another forty minutes, he had built a clear picture of the young woman.

* * *

His retching echoed within the toilet bowl and although he felt nauseous, the dry heaving was purely a reaction to the emotional trauma, a trauma of his own making. He spat into the bowl as if trying to expel whatever self-disgust he had experienced, before moving through into the lounge. His trembling hand poured a large scotch into a heavy tumbler before a single cube of ice was added. It was smooth as he allowed the liquid to run around his mouth in the hope it would perform some sort of catharsis. As he swallowed the liquid, it warmed, and he immediately felt better. Only then did he move to the framed photographs. He selected one, a favourite, but one that was always positioned towards the back of the few that sat on the bookshelves filling one wall of the room. The silver frame, bright and mirrorlike, trapped the image against a blue velvet background. The laughing face seemed alive, petrified at the moment the shutter had been pushed. His mind flicked immediately to the face. His hand began to shake the tumbler as his whole body trembled and convulsed. Tears ran down his cheeks and his watery vision blurred the mental image as he tried to focus on the beauty of the photograph he held.

'Why?'

It was only one word, but the retaliatory anger was clear should anyone have been able to hear. The counsellor, the psych, had told him it was a normal response, it was only human and that time would help, as would the medication. Grieving affects people differently, but he seemed to have had more than his fair share. The professional support and guidance had often brought greater confusion than healing. Throughout his earlier life, he had never been an angry person. Yes, things had troubled him, but usually only for a short period. He found that work often diffused the frustrations of his life. Even after his separation, he did not feel anger towards either her or her lovers, quickly realising that it was all part of life. Life could often throw down obstacles. He also knew that his work ethic, a self-induced pattern, was not conducive to a normal relationship, if any relationship could fall into the normal category.

There would have been a time this glass would have been a bottle but, in a relatively short space of time and with the right guidance, he had drawn a halt to the destructive traits that gnawed at his very core. He had realised that being out of control would lead to only one ending, an ending that would arrive too soon. Glancing back at the photograph, it was one of the reasons he had crashed off the rails in the first instance, yet memories became his liberator and salvation. He had chosen a path hoping for salvation and redemption, but it only seemed to have brought disgust. He placed the photograph to his lips and kissed the glass, wondering how many lives it would take to feel satiated, to feel compensated. Closing his eyes, he hoped it would come sooner rather than later.

Sitting down, he allowed his eyes to close. Photographs and videos swirled in his mind's eye, a mass of media that replayed, a mental recording interrupting his sleep, disturbing and often de-railing his working day, until he knew every single frame, every person in it and every captured movement. It was his only reason to persevere, to get better, and in some ways, this was his only mission in life. He swirled the ice within the amber fluid and watched as it created its own Charybdis, and within that simple action, it calmed his own inner, psychological monster. That and the sound of the ice against the side of the glass brought a distracting relief. A book lay on the coffee table, his book, a novel that would allow him to forget for a while. Leaning over, he picked it up, after moving Caitlin's mobile phone. He found the bookmark and allowed himself time to suspend his disbelief.

* * *

Michael checked the time; it was just after 10.30. He nibbled a Tunnock's wafer as he checked Caitlin's details. Considering her place of employment, he presumed that she would still be at work. Picking up the phone after referring again to his list, he tapped in the number of Blakey's Restaurant. It rang only twice.

'Blakey's, Hugo speaking. How may I help you?' There was a weariness in the response, it sounded almost automated.

'Hi, sorry it's late. Could I speak with Caitlin please? I'm a good friend.'

There was a pause, and Michael could hear the noise of the room in the background. 'You could if she still worked here. She no longer does.'

'She told me—'

'From earlier today. She was finished, sacked if that doesn't sound too brutal. Her services were no longer required. For your information, and I speak to you in confidence as her friend, she was late in work and not for the first time. We try to run a successful business and not a rehab service for people who cannot take their responsibilities seriously. If, as you say, you are her friend, may I politely suggest you have a strong word with her. She's a talented waitress, but … Now, if there's nothing else I can do for you, sir, I have much to do here as we are a staff member short.'

'No, no. Thanks, I shall talk to her when I see her. Thank you for your trust and honesty.'

Michael put down the phone. He wanted to inform Hugo politely as a riposte that people are not always perfect and, in fact, there was even a snake in the Garden of Eden but thought it unwise. He did have some sympathy as he, too, abhorred tardiness, especially in a professional sense; he always had. Noting the time and the details of the call, he jotted a note and sent it to both Skeeter and April. Conscious now of the time, he called Control requesting a patrol attend her address as soon as possible to see if she were home.

Within the hour he had been notified that she was not answering the door. The time was now 11.22. He requested they check again in another hour.

In his mind, there was something that clearly did not gel. His last resort would be to use the created Facebook page, to post the 'Friend' request and hope it would either be accepted or rejected. One way or the other, he needed an answer. All he could do now was to be patient and wait.

CHAPTER 11

The early morning darkness lingered as April inspected the finished stained glass against the artificial light. It had taken her longer than she had anticipated, having to return to it after enjoying the hotpot supper she had received from Sue. Allowing the warm light to shine through it convinced her the extra time had been worth the effort. The multiple varied facets of the glass surfaces sparkled as she moved it in her hands. She was pleased with the coruscation of contrasting colours, the way the shapes and texture of the glass surfaces brought the piece to life. Tico yawned, less impressed than April, and stood at the other side of the child gate, a necessary safeguard to keep sensitive paws away from any fine glass splinters on the studio floor.

She lay the artwork on the bench, enjoying a final glance before taking Tico for a walk on the beach, and then she would head out to work.

* * *

The night had been long, but he was pleased his alcohol intake had been restricted to one glass. That simple act of abstinence had brought, along with the early night, a clear head. Looking at the shafts of sunlight needling through the blinds convinced him he should go for a run, just as he had done each day when his evening's alcohol intake had been controlled. Besides, he needed an isolated location before switching on Caitlin's phone. If her body had been found, there was every chance the police would be tracking it.

Once down Blucher Street, he passed the junction of Adelaide Terrace and Beach Lawn before crossing the grassed area directly before the Crosby coastline. As usual, he turned and ran towards Crosby Promenade. The wind always seemed to catch him off guard, but the disturbance brought a salty freshness. Once on the pathway, the Gormley figures were clearly visible, well-spaced and yet semi-silhouetted against the silver sparkle of the sea. Here was the reason to live, to survive. The flat watery expanse seemed like a vast sheet of buffed aluminium that concealed the horizon, perfectly blending sea with sky. Pausing, he rested his hands on his knees and bent to take deep breaths as his eyes fell on the Burbo Bank Wind Farm that was lost in the morning gloom. Removing Caitlin's phone, he tapped in the passcode he had created, and the morning immediately became more interesting; a Facebook friend request had arrived overnight. It raised a smile and made the hairs on his neck tingle. *Had they found her or was this just a co-incidence?* His thoughts raced bringing a frisson of excitement. He talked to himself in a whisper. 'Now that is what I would have done. It's amazing just what you can discover when you have the knowledge.'

Either way, he looked at the request with great interest and a degree of circumspection. It was vital that he consider the intro posted and the number of mutual friends shown. Those elements would make a difference.

* * *

For Michael, the digital forensic technicians had created a perfect page adding a number of mutual friends and forming a basic introduction. The header was a picture of someone singing into a mic.

* * *

'Now what would Caitlin do, @MicKnight, dance to your tune?' he asked, speaking out loud as he studied the image, his words lost to the onshore breeze. He scratched his forehead and with no further consideration tapped 'confirm request'. He would now wait to see if further communication would follow. Somehow, he had his doubts but if it did, he would progress with caution. He switched off the phone.

* * *

Once home, he showered, finished the mug of coffee that was best described as tepid, selected a hat, checked for the face covering and picked up the tote bag placed by the door. The red hood it contained would soon be disposed of. His morning run had offered up the perfect location.

* * *

April paused as she approached her desk. The envelope attached to her computer screen made her smile. She knew immediately Michael had been working hard. Peeling away the folded tape from the screen surround, she withdrew two sheets of A4. As always, it was handwritten in a neat, cursive script.

Good morning, April,

The eagle has landed. Caitlin has accepted the friend request we made. I've added a screenshot of her opening page. The tech people did a great job in setting up the false account. There has been no further communication, but we now have a twenty-four-hour watch on the phone. Before I left, it was tracked to the Crosby area remaining active for four minutes ending at 6.14! Asked for CCTV of the area but there's a lot of open land at that point along the coastline. She could also have been indoors or in a vehicle.

What Caitlin would be doing, quite some distance from her home address, is unknown. Interestingly, that time contradicts other information I received about her. As you might have seen from a mail I sent earlier, I called her known place of work. It's on file as you're aware. According to Hugo, the manager, she was fired for poor timekeeping and did not work yesterday. From his report, she tends to make it a regular thing so being out and about before seven in the morning made me wonder. I requested a further home visit at 7.22 as I was getting ready to leave. Detailed are the previous two visits made that were unsuccessful. Hopefully, they will have contacted her by now if she's home.

Always glad to be of assistance. As you read this, I shall be dreaming of sunshine and beaches ... and before you think it, not Crosby!!

Best,

Nocturnal Michael

April checked the added screenshot. As if on cue, her desk phone rang. There was a brief introduction.

'We've been directed to you, ma'am. There are again no signs that Caitlin Byrne is at home. The neighbours who live above saw her leave yesterday evening but not return and they have neither seen nor heard anything since. A friend called, her name's Steph and the only details they have for her is her mobile number. At Steph's request, the neighbour went and knocked but there was no response. As I said, the friend left her contact details with the neighbour. There is real concern. According to the neighbour, although Caitlin is not the most reliable individual, this is not her usual behaviour.'

April paused. 'Her phone was switched on briefly early this morning. She might be out. Does the neighbour have or know of someone there who might have a key to the apartment? A landlord?'

'It's an owned flat. We've checked with her neighbours in the block, but it seems more unlikely.' The officer's intonation seemed to suggest they were wasting time, and she was probably out, maybe all night.

'Check with the neighbour to see the direction she went last night.' The phone was muted as the officer asked the question. April waited, tapping her fingers on the desk.

'Mrs Fellows, the neighbour, saw her cross the road. She was wearing a coat and went into the general store. However, she was watching telly and didn't see her leave the shop. Neither did she hear her return. Her husband is a bit deaf, and the volume is raised.' The officer sighed.

Had April been able to see the officer's facial expression she would have clearly seen the tiredness. The officers attending thought they were on a wild goose chase. If she could read their minds, she would have been shocked to learn their view that if they chased every young, single female who did not come home after a night out, they would vanish up their own backsides. Fortunately, that gem was denied.

April was like a dog with a bone. 'Question those in the shop. CCTV. Sometimes they have an external camera. Let me know as soon as.'

April could not tolerate their laissez-faire attitude, even though she knew the officers attending were at the end of their long shift. She had experienced it more frequently with the younger officers, particularly at the start and end of their working day.

Tony tapped on the door and his face appeared. 'I've seen Michael's report. I'm concerned. Don't know why but something's not right. She's there on the video and then she disappears. I don't like coincidences, never have. I've checked with the phone company and from the records her phone is rarely switched off.' He stepped forward and folded his arms, the concern clearly showing on his face.

'Your concern is shared. Her good friend is also worried. If I'm not happy when I hear back from the officers at her flat … then.'

'A warrant?' Tony knew there was no need if they had evidence to suggest someone's life or limb was in danger.

April's phone rang again. Tony watched for telltale signs on her face as to the information she was digesting.

'Wine and crisps? Do we have a time?' She picked up a pen, jotting down the information. 'And when she left?' April turned and looked at Tony. 'Thanks. Yes, request the CCTV.'

Tony leaned against one of the panels in the glass wall.

'According to the shop owner, she was in the store briefly. According to the time on the CCTV, entering at 19.26 leaving at 19.33. The images suggest she crossed the road, so at this stage we must assume that she was returning to the flat. There's an outside camera on the shop and the images will be sent over. I want Scene of Crimes in as soon as, Tony. Contact the upper neighbours and let them know we're coming. There's no need for officers to break through all the doors in the place. Once Control has sorted that, I want you there and fast to organise. Report back as soon as. Let's just hope she's had a heavy night and couldn't be roused.'

Moving swiftly to the door, Tony made his way to his desk, collected his things and organised a car. As always, too much time was involved in dealing with procedures. It would take eighteen minutes with the strobe lights and horns. The tactical unit would be a little longer.

* * *

Alan Green waited in the usual place. He exhaled huge clouds of vapour after drawing on the e-cigarette, a machine that bore no resemblance to its name. He watched as the ethereal fumes dissipated into disparate, wispy patterns before vanishing completely. The cigarette's tank holding the vaping liquid seemed disproportionately large. The atomiser, the heating coil that releases the trapped nicotine and flavours, had been adjusted to create the strongest burn, resulting in a bigger hit and a large plume, a cloud that seemed cotton wool white as it hovered briefly around his head. He tried to end the ritual by blowing a smoke ring but as usual he failed miserably.

It was always the same location; the orders were clear. To stand by the post box at the gate of Anchor Courtyard at the far end of the Albert Dock at the set time. To Alan it was the most difficult place to get to: he had to walk further than he liked; it was always full of people at the designated time and often the wind was cutting. Leaning on the post box, he glanced at the Ferris wheel positioned a short distance across the narrow stretch of water. The upper part was smudged colourless by a layer of mist that had loitered all morning, spreading out from the centre of the river giving the whole machine a ghostly appearance. He yawned as his phone rang. He fumbled trying to locate it. He waited for the second ring and, as usual, it stopped. He looked around knowing the caller was somewhere, looking, watching. It rang again. He suddenly felt anxious.

CHAPTER 12

The two officers who had originally been called to attend Caitlin's flat had followed instructions and strung police tape strategically across the pavement to keep the public away from the front of the apartments. Even in the daylight, the blue flash of the strobe lights bounced off the buildings, announcing a police presence. It was always a siren's call to the nosey and the curious … and, in this neighbourhood particularly, they had come, congregating and asking the usual questions or making what they believed to be witty, original, anti-police comments. The mobile phones also appeared to capture the scene, not that there was much to see. The officers had heard many of the comments before but occasionally some Scouse originality about the force raised a smile. Cars travelling down Stanley Road slowed, curious heads turning to catch a glimpse. Within seconds, the special unit, two officers carrying the tools needed to make short work of opening closed doors, moved equipment from the side of a van and entered the building as Tony monitored the front door. Mrs Fellows had followed instructions and retreated upstairs. She watched and listened on the landing. As the officers passed, Tony glanced at their visored helmets, each having the letters SU, followed by their individual identification number, stencilled clearly in contrasting yellow on blue. They were heavily protected as they were never sure as to what might be waiting on the other side of the door. Another officer followed holding a gimballed camera recording their every action.

They swung the large, red enforcer, sixteen kilograms of steel, against the door lock; it offered little resistance. The loud splintering of wood echoed throughout the hallway. It took only one strike, and within moments they entered giving a loud warning.

'Police!' bawled the first officer to enter. The two others followed in swift succession, before immediately pausing at the scene that greeted them. Caitlin's prostrate figure was clearly visible. Tony, observing from the shattered door, called for immediate medical back-up. One of the officers pulled out a cut-down tool from his vest – a hook-shaped plastic tool that had its blade encased in a protective guard, so it was impossible for it to be used to slash or stab. It was designed only to cut through a rope or ligature. It made short work of the electrician's tie and within seconds, the bag was removed. A thin film of moisture was seen to cover Caitlin's pale, gaunt face. The officer's gloved hand searched for a pulse but there was nothing. It was also clear to him that rigor mortis had set in.

'Air ambulance, five minutes. Landing on the park,' Tony called as he moved just into the room.

One officer raised a hand and shook his head. 'She's been dead some time.'

The helicopter's arrival had already been organised as additional officers had secured the landing site on Bootle Park. Tony considered cancelling the flight but knew the craft would now be close. The critical care air ambulance team would be able to confirm the death. He also called for CSIs to be present. In Tony's mind, there was a possibility he could be looking at a suicide, but his gut doubted that hypothesis. He dialled April as the air ambulance team moved into the room and waited for an initial response before pressing the call button.

'The doctor believes she's been dead between three and five hours but that's only an approximation at this time. As we know, it can never be definitive.'

April responded as Tony watched the medics clearing away their equipment. 'Suicide, Tony?'

Tony moved down the steps to the front of the flats. 'To be honest, in my opinion, she hasn't done this herself. CSIs are now present. I'm treating it as murder until evidence proves to the contrary.'

Tony breathed fresh air. He heard the helicopter's rotor, loud and rhythmic, as the crash of the blades' tips sliced the air. The sound was amplified as it bounced off the buildings surrounding him. He watched its graceful, curling flight, lights blinking, as it headed back to Blackpool.

April spoke. 'We've contacted her friend, Steph. She's confirmed Caitlin managed to land a new job yesterday after losing her old one ... The reason she went for wine. According to this friend, Caitlin sounded very positive and upbeat, so evidence suggests she was certainly not suicidal.'

* * *

Alan Green followed the instructions he had received. Halftide Wharf seemed miles away but in fact, it was less than a mile and his expression demonstrated his reluctance to walk. It would take him ten minutes at best. He would have dearly loved to have grabbed one of the many e-scooters, but that idea had been frowned upon since he had joined the OAA gang, letters of a chosen postcode. The scooters were easily tracked via GPS and many now had cameras linked to AI.

The caller had explained what a capstan was and had given specific details of its location. Within four minutes, he saw it, closer than he had expected and it was where indicated – set on what appeared to be a block paved island positioned at kerb height from the road and protected by steel, black bollards and other metal items. The litter was as described, too, stuffed in the numerous square holes that ran around the metal ring at the top. He moved an empty bottle and looked inside. The envelope trapped within a plastic bag was stuffed behind a crushed coke can.

Opening the sealed bag with his teeth, he tore along the top of the envelope. The small wad of twenty-pound notes was there as promised, as well as a further instruction. It was typed. He now had the next set of orders, and he felt a faint tingle of excitement flutter in his stomach. For the third time, it had been easy money, and no questions were asked. His phone rang again. No number showed as usual.

'I see you have the package.' The Scouse accent was strong as always; somehow, he thought he was a *plazee*, a professional Scouser, an actor, but the thought quickly evaporated.

Alan scanned the area, the river to his back limited the vicinity he needed to check. 'Ta, yes. Capstan, seen 'em before but didn't know they were called that.'

'Good. Get your lads ready. The date is on the note. As previously, I need nothing from you. Anything collected is for you.' The call ended.

Alan shook his head. The word *nutter* had gone through his mind a number of times. He sat on the capstan and reflected on their first contact. He inhaled the vapour from his e-cigarette and wondered who this invisible benefactor might be. He thought he had seen him at the jobs, but he could not be certain.

Alan watched the vapour slowly disappear. It was very much like the mysterious man; he was like smoke. Tapping his pocket, he took another look around before heading back towards the Albert Dock.

* * *

Tony looked across at Skeeter as he entered, tossing his coat onto his chair. The extent of his despondency was clear.

'You look as though you need a brew!' She stood, leaning on the edge of her desk. 'I've received all the details from April. Why do I have the feeling she's an innocent victim?'

'There's something not right. Our victim is on video at a crime scene one day and then she's the main focus of—' Tony pulled a face, unable to comprehend what he had just witnessed. 'A brew did you say? Christ, yes.' He sank onto his chair. 'No matter how many times you see death, Wicca, it never gets any easier.'

Skeeter placed the mug on his desk and slid a chocolate biscuit next to it. 'You look as though you could do with a sugar rush.' She leaned on the blue dividing screen. 'The friend request Michael posted was accepted early doors today on her Facebook page. Strangely, she was dead well before that according to the attending medic.'

'The killer has her phone,' Tony uttered without any surprise in his voice. 'I'll tell you what else, Wicca, he's bloody testing us. This is all plotted. You mark my words.'

'Or she. Go on.'

'Whoever it is, whatever sex or gender they might like to identify as, they know that we have now linked the robbery with her.'

Skeeter frowned, cupped her eyes and began to rub them gently. 'No, Tony, they've allowed us to. There was no reason why they should respond to the request, to accept it. It was, in my eyes, sore as they may be, a subtle yet deliberate move on their part.'

Tony pushed the remaining biscuit into his mouth. 'It's not a game.' He looked at her. 'Or is it?' He scratched his forehead before picking up his mug.

* * *

Alan Green sat in KFC, the drink of Coke was all he had left of his meal, apart from the wrappers. His finger found his right nostril, drilled gently but deeply for a few moments before withdrawing and inspecting what had been mined. He quickly rolled it between finger and thumb, and almost without thinking, flicked it away. It landed on the edge of the table. He removed the envelope from his pocket. Leaving the money, he took out the note. Reading was not and never had been one of his strong points, but he could manage to comprehend the majority of written words.

Well done! I hope what you took proved profitable, Mr Green.

I would like the same group. This time, we hunt a bigger fish. Think about the tools you will need to go through the front window. Check it! You will have to be quick. In and out with no messing. Whatever you take is yours, plus my same cash prize. Hoods, red hoods, are essential. King's Ransom Pawn Broker's and Jeweller's, Whitechapel. Time must be just after 10 and before 10.15. Neither be earlier nor late. The window will be full at that time. I strongly advise you not to arrive earlier. As always, Greenie, my boy, I'll be watching so make sure there are no cockups.

Now plan and plan well. I'll be in touch in the usual way.

Alan read the note a few more times, and even though he knew the location, he checked on his phone for the map of Whitechapel, realising quickly that this was going to be far more difficult than the previous two jobs. He grabbed his drink, tipped his head back and drained it before crushing it in his hand.

CHAPTER 13

K asum studied the CCTV footage of the other known motorcycle shoplifting incidents that had taken place within the previous six months. They had all been investigated but with no success, if no one was hurt, there seemed little enthusiasm to maintain a dedicated investigation. The thin blue line was just that. She had also studied the case of the death of a pedestrian robbed in daylight by a single bike but there was no CCTV of the incident. She checked the file carefully and although an appeal to the public had been made, no dashcam footage had been received. She had, however, organised some still images taken from the shop attacks and they were now attached to the whiteboards. She also ran the full CCTV footage of the incidents, watching them at half speed on the large screen positioned in the now increasingly busy Incident Room.

She paused the shot as they were watching the third of four. A smile came to her lips. Enlarging the image, she looked at the figure in the hat and the medical mask. It was not as clear as she would have liked. Turning to her colleagues, she tapped the still image attached to the whiteboard. She said nothing but their eyes moved between the screen and the board.

'Different but the same. Gender?'

There was a pause but eventually a consensus. 'Male, the appearance of a male we can assume?' There were nods of agreement. 'Now when I pan out, tell me what else you notice.'

'There are some people using their phones to capture the incident.' DC Phil Lipson answered with a degree of excitement. 'That's not the girl—'.

'No, Phil, that would be far too convenient. Ask yourself, however, did we check the social media posts immediately after these events?' She did not give them time to respond. 'The answer is no. Why? Because the crime was shoplifting, petty crime, and at that stage, there was no evidence to suggest they were gang related and, importantly, nobody was hurt. As you know, this is happening in every town and city in the UK far too regularly, and if nobody is hurt, attacked or injured then—'

'We hope it solves itself?' Lucy spoke neither wishing to sound flippant nor callous.

Kasum frowned. 'Indeed. Now we have a possible murder linked to one of these many crimes, which could mean there's something else we might have missed. Are they linked, connected in some way?' There was a pause, it gave her a few moments to think as the frown returned to her face. 'In the footage of the earlier robberies there are no hoods, just black balaclava-type ski masks.' She picked up the remote. 'Look at this one, the one prior to the latest robbery.' She paused it and turned to the group.

'Hoods! They're wearing what could be best described as individual red hoods,' someone said from the back of the room.

'You should be a detective,' Phil called. Laughter erupted but died away quickly.

'Patchwork faces are only to the front of the hoods but on the latest attack, they were sewn to the front as well as the back. It's as if the gang is developing, mutating.'

Kasum nodded. 'Can we assume they are one and the same group?'

'The bikes look the same,' Phil announced.

'What, black and electric?' the officer standing next to him quipped. 'Polar bears look identical but they're not.'

Phil turned, a huge frown on his face. 'Bugger off. You know what I mean. They strip them to the bare minimum. Probably all nicked or sourced from the same place, the black market.'

'Thank you.' Kasum looked sternly at both men. 'April believes they're one and the same gang and she also feels, but has no evidence to support this, they're working up to something more audacious.'

'Like murder?' Lucy offered with a seriousness that brought a pause.

'Let's hope that's not prophetic, Lucy,' Kasum replied as she looked up.

'Tony Price came up with the theory that the hoods identify the players, the man in the pictures, Joe Public, is the coach, The Controller. Some of the gang will be selected for certain jobs whilst others …'

Phil waved a hand. 'You mentioned that the people using their phones to record the earlier incidents were not checked, their socials and stuff and yet now we have a dead woman who did the same. Should we be checking back if that's at all possible?'

'Bingo!' Kasum turned to Lucy. 'Please check dates and times and get the technical forensics to work their magic.'

* * *

Skeeter and Tony were on time to meet Steph. It was her lunch break. They hoped the news of Caitlin's death had not reached her. Agreeing to meet in a quiet café just around the corner from her office they had watched her enter and swiftly scan the room. Tony stood.

She lifted a hand and moved over to their table. Skeeter sensed from the look in her eyes that she had an inkling bad news was about to be divulged.

'Thank you for coming. I'm DC Price and my colleague, DS Warlock. Can I get you a coffee?'

She nodded. 'Thanks, a skinny flat white.'

Steph looked at Skeeter, her reaction was that of many when seeing her for the first time. The marked contrast in her eyes, the slightly crooked nose, the tightly plaited hair and the cauliflower ear gave her a harsh appearance. Tony returned with her coffee and sat.

'Do you have bad news? I told Mark, he's my boyfriend, I said I had a funny feeling. Is it bad? I've had this churning in my stomach since going to her flat, intuition probably, that things were not right. We've been friends for ages.' She looked up and then at each officer in turn, as if watching a tennis match, not knowing from whom the answer might come. Her eyes fell on Skeeter. The pause seemed agonisingly long.

'I'm sorry but we do have bad news.' Skeeter spoke without any emotion. The sounds of the café seemed to disappear, the calm before the storm. 'I'm afraid she's dead.'

It was as if the flood gates had been breached and tears flowed down Steph's cheeks. Tears that had been held back through hope, were now accompanied with a loud cry. A number of customers turned but quickly looked away as Skeeter matched their stare. Skeeter leaned forward and rested a reassuring hand on Steph's. She waited for her to regain a degree of control.

'We're sorry, that was tough. We've notified her next of kin. We wanted to see you before it appears in the news.'

'Maggie, how's Maggie, her mum, bless her? Her dad left

home a couple of years back. Caitlin had left before that, and she was devastated that her family had crumbled. If I'm truthful, I don't think mother and daughter were as close as they liked to imply. I said that to—'

It was as if she were speaking quickly to hide her distress. Skeeter raised a hand. She stopped mid-sentence.

'Sorry, I thought ...' Steph looked back at the coffee.

'Next of kin have been informed.' Tony repeated.

'We need to establish exactly what happened last night. So, let's take it step by step and consider her movements over the last couple of days.'

Tony slipped his phone on the table to record the conversation.

'She lost her job. She was dead upset but then she found another the same day, it was only yesterday. That's so like her. One minute she was in the trough of despair and the next as high as a kite. That's Caitlin. She called me to say come round as she was buying wine, but she also said she was having an early night. That's Caitlin all over! She was a confused mess, but she was beautiful.'

Tony, whilst also making notes, asked without lifting his head. 'When did you last see her?'

'Wednesday, yes, Wednesday. We met for drinks with another friend, Jan. It was her day off. It's funny but she was wasted very quickly. We took her home in a taxi and put her to bed, made sure she was safe, and the taxi driver helped us. He was brilliant. Found out later she'd been at it before she came out. A couple, she'd said but her measures were always, how can I say it, extremely generous.'

Skeeter turned to look at Tony and then back at Steph.

'How did you book the taxi?' Skeeter asked.

'The Uber app on my phone.'

'How did you leave the flat, the key?'

'We put her keys on her bag and dropped the latch. You don't need a key to leave through the front door as it has an electronic thingy.'

Tony made a note as no keys, as far as he was aware, had been located in the flat.

'Was it unusual for her to get so intoxicated?' Skeeter asked whilst folding her hands before propping them beneath her chin. The comment brought a laugh, the first change in Steph's demeanour since her arrival.

'God, no. She's part Irish and she knows how to party. She's danced on many a tab—' Tears came again. 'Sorry.'

Skeeter grabbed a napkin from a pot at the end of the table and slipped it to her. 'What did she talk about before she …?'

Steph blew her nose. 'She'd witnessed a shoplifting, motorbikes and stuff. You see it on the socials all the time. She showed us her video. She was proud of it. Told us she'd posted it. She always wanted to be famous, but partying was all she was really good at. That brings the wrong sort of attention, and she's had her fair share of idiots.'

Tony looked up and then back at his notes.

'Did she say anything about that incident she'd seen?' Skeeter enquired.

There was a pause. Steph blew her nose again and nodded. 'Yes, we told her she'd found an admirer.' It was then she stopped and looked directly at Skeeter. The frown on her face said everything.

CHAPTER 14

Alan Green sat on wooden pallets. The headlight clipped to his bobble hat spread a wide beam reaching to the surfaces of the extended cavernous space. The roughly hewn stone walls were grey-blue. The space always brought his grandfather to mind as he banged on about The Cavern, the Beatles and all that was good about Liverpool in the sixties. He was like a broken record that never seemed to end as he wittered on and on. This space was different. He had known it since he was a kid. It appeared inaccessible, certainly hidden and yet now it was not as exclusive as it once had been. At the end of the previous year, some urban explorers had found it and posted images on the internet under the title, *The Eye of the Earth* and *The Dragon's Eye*. That had been a pain in the arse as it suddenly became the place to find. Fortunately, the explorers had left the true location out of their posts but still, from the videos posted on YouTube, some adventurous teenagers had located it, although the local residents had soon put a stop to that.

Sitting above him was the reason for the attention: the eye. Caught in the diffused artificial light, it was clear to see, captured when the torchlight shone at a certain angle, flushing the huge circular shape within the mine's ceiling. It was a geological anomaly, a freak of the natural world that had quickly been interpreted to represent a huge eye – watchful, secretive, a wyvern's cyclopic gaze. Although magnificent when the light was right, it could also be quite sinister. On the ground, directly below the convex orb, were the remnants of the delaminated layer of rock that had broken away leaving another natural phenomenon. Leached water that had caused the fall had stained the roof in patterns: slate blue with contrasting marbling of orange and veined with white, rust red from the calcium sulphate and iron that had been carried in the water. Liquid had percolated through the rock's minute fissures over many years, forming the myriad patterns, bringing not only a realism to the eye, but a magnificence to the ceiling.

The echo of another person startled him, but the reassuring metallic tap on one of the passageway's concrete geodetic-like pillars was the calling card he wanted to hear. The fast-moving beam of light flashed, bounced, disappeared before returning and growing ever stronger as they approached. Alan tapped the metal rod he held against the stone by his feet.

'Greenie!' the hollow voice called from somewhere in the darkness. 'Bloody hell, seems to take longer each time. My dad always said I was crap at directions. Took a wrong turn where it says, "Welcome to Hell".'

Their own graffiti daubed in red, runny paint, had been written to frighten and deter young kids.

'I always go bloody left instead of right.'

'As long as you don't go down the slope before the cross-roads, Smigga, as that's the way to Hades, to hell!' Alan tried his best horror movie voice followed by a laugh but failed miserably.

'Fuck off, tosser!'

A solitary figure emerged, and Alan Green was temporarily blinded by the torchlight. He shielded his eyes.

'Where's Sparra?' A nickname acquired on account of his thin legs.

Smigga just raised his shoulders. 'Fuck knows.'

Moments later they both turned, hearing the tap, the signal. Turning off their lights they awaited the appearance of the solitary, bouncing beam. Sparra quickly approached before tucking his torch below his chin, the light flooding the front of his face, distorting his features with the contrasting shadows.

'That's a vast improvement, Sparra. Stop buggering about, you're late.'

'Dog walker in the woods near the entrance. Thought it wise to give him time to bugger off, like.'

The other two lights came on, illuminating the vaulted space. 'Good thinking.' Alan spoke with a degree of frustration. 'Let's get on.'

* * *

For the first time since her coffee arrived, Steph picked her cup up, sipping as she held it with both hands. 'When we told Cat she had an admirer, she told us she hadn't noticed him. I suppose she was more focused on the chaos that was going on inside.'

Tony pushed three photographs, taken from the CCTV footage across the table – not from Caitlin's social media – of the man they believed to be part of the group. 'Is this the man?'

Steph studied each carefully and nodded. 'Yes, I've not seen these before, Caitlin's was …' She looked up at Skeeter who nodded.

'Thank you. This is not from that incident. What about

yesterday and the job issues?' Tony quizzed, realising they had reached a dead end with the last question.

'Hugo sacked her. Jan had phoned early in the morning to check on her, but she didn't pick up, so she was obviously hung over.' She took another sip of her flat white. 'Goodness knows what time she got to work. She's a jammy bugger. Sacked before lunch and employed again by the afternoon, an Irish bar, she said it was.'

'Any idea which one?' Skeeter asked; a few she had frequented came to mind.

Steph shook her head. 'She also said she was chatted up by some bloke but that's all. I don't know where that was or when, probably a bar at lunchtime, knowing her. Probably called in for a drink to drown her sorrows.' She checked her watch. 'Must get back, although to be honest, I feel like curling up in a dark room. Hope I've been of help. I still can't believe it. Do we know when the funeral will be?'

Skeeter shook her head. 'No, the family will keep you informed. If anything else comes to mind, no matter how ridiculous you feel it might be, please call this number.' Tony slipped a card across the table. 'We appreciate your time and again, we're sorry for your loss. You'll see it announced in the local press and the news shortly. Probably Caitlin's photograph, too, and her video of the robbery, which may well show the man in question.' Tony nodded and Steph took the signal to go. She stood, forced a smile and left.

'I'll get the calls to all the Irish bars.' Skeeter removed her phone, tapped on Google Maps and searched Blakey's restaurant. She then searched, Irish bars in that locality. 'I'll get calls in to each one.'

* * *

'Sorry, Greenie. I also had a bit of an issue at home, but it's sorted.' Sparra pulled a face that gave little clue as to the cause of his problem and changed the subject. 'Is it only me but this place never seems to get cold. You think it'd be cold and damp.' His eyes fell on them both, but the only answer came from Alan.

'Used to store ammunition during World War Two from all accounts. Made the stuff in Kirkby, stored it here. That's why there's huge steel doors on the other side of the hill in the old house's back garden, a quarry or mine of some kind before that. Safest place to store explosives, apparently. The tunnels go on for some distance, but some have collapsed since when I was a nipper. I know there are some deep voids, too, so you have to be especially careful. Anyroad up, we have another job. Not easy, yet no trouble for us OAA lads. We'll have to be sharp, though, no fucking about like one of us did last time.' He slapped Smigga across his hat. 'No trespassing indoors on two bloody wheels, like.'

Sparra sniggered.

'Bloody class that was.' Smigga smirked. 'Fucking pure riding skill.'

Nothing else was said as Alan removed bundles of money from his inner pocket. In total, it was a percentage of the payment he had received, shared out fairly. 'The eye of the earth is witness to the fact you're getting paid. It's with thanks from the Bossman. Pass on half to your passengers. This next job is the same terms, what we snatch, we keep … plus … a bigger fee. Win, win.'

There was an audible grumble from Smigga as the money was being counted by the others.

'It's all there,' Green's sharp tongue was quick to announce.

'Who the fuck is he anyway. Takes now't, just pays out and for what? Doesn't seem right to me, what says you Sparra?'

'Providing this comes, I don't give a flying fook.' Sparra

kissed the notes before folding them and stuffing them into his coat pocket.

'Now, out one at a time and await the call. Remember, the locals keep an eye open since this place hit the internet. If you're stopped, be polite.' The two nodded their understanding. 'Remember you could be looking for your lost dog.' He grinned.

Alan waited, watching the light of their torches slowly disappear whilst their muffled voices still echoed. He would leave last and ensure the narrow, barred entrance they had all squeezed through was secured. Once the lights had disappeared, he shone his head lamp towards the mine's roof. The huge eye, the dragon's eye, came into focus. He stared at it for a few moments; it was clearly reptilian. His thoughts turned to the Bossman and the particular way in which he spoke, the plastic Scouser who seemed to see all but want nothing. The question, 'Why?' flooded his mind and the more he thought, the more uncomfortable he felt. 'Could the man be a snake in the grass?' he said to himself. For the first time since his arrival, he suddenly sensed a chill.

Growing up, he had often tested himself, challenged himself to overcome fear. If people said he could not do something, he did it no matter how long it took. That's why people followed, listened and in many ways feared him. His temper took time to simmer, but when it did, he blew. The chill quickly wrapped around him and he physically shivered. He took one long, defiant look at the eye and realised it was time for him to leave.

* * *

The PCC press office had formulated the news regarding the murder and the link with the robbery to be broadcast. Images of the individual and close up pictures of the hoods accompanied the posts. They were expecting a full and swift response from the public.

Skeeter had received a call from the station to say they had located the Irish bar and both she and Tony turned back towards the city centre.

* * *

Cillian looked up as soon as they entered and pointed a finger in recognition of the company he was expecting. There was a smell of stale beer that always seemed to linger within the atmosphere. and even though smoking was not permitted, a gossamer haze seemed to accompany the aroma. Dark wood, polished floors, mirrors and framed pictures filled one wall, juxtaposed randomly with objects and traditional musical instruments. Green seemed to be the dominant colour. A few early punters were sitting around; a couple of men nursing pints had their eyes fixed to the large wall flatscreen, engrossed in the horse racing. The décor could well be described as cluttered.

'For sure, I was expecting you, just as I was expecting the young lady, Caitlin, about whom the officer spoke on the phone. Now, I suppose, these days two out of three can't be that bad.' Cillian smiled. 'Can I be getting either of you a drink; non-alcoholic, of course?' He stared at Skeeter as Tony introduced her. 'You'll not be a relation of the old archbishop would you, by some chance, for if you are you could put in a good word for me?'

'Different spelling, different religion but the same philosophy to law, peace and goodwill.' She winked the darker eye, bringing a frown to Cillian's face.

The tune of 'When Irish Eyes are Smiling' came briefly to his mind and he realised it was not a look of love she had proffered. 'That settles that. What can I be doing for you, then?'

They went through his meeting with Caitlin, quizzing him about his whereabouts at the time of her death but it was clear he had been in the bar until late. Despite his ebullient manner, it was also very clear to Skeeter that he was, behind his façade, still clearly shocked at the news, even though he had only had the briefest of meetings with Caitlin.

'You just never know these days. There are some evil bastards hanging around in plain sight, we see our fair share in here. It's frightening what the booze can do to people. Your jobs must be a bloody nightmare at times, as in the eyes of many, you can't often do right for doing wrong.' He focused on Skeeter as he spoke.

'Pachyderm-like skin is what they make us grow during basic training. Usually the more people protest, the more guilt they're trying to hide. Thanks for your co-operation.' She never let her face slip as she turned to leave.

Within minutes, they were back in the car.

'That closes that avenue,' Tony grumbled.

'We'll see, Tony, we'll see.'

CHAPTER 15

The briefing room was busy as people checked the information they had received to date. The room, although modern, was deliberately sparse. April tapped the table with a drumstick, and someone was heard to add the cymbal sound 'tich'. April's eyes scanned the room but failed to identify the culprit or the funny side.

'I attended the prelim pathology on Caitlin Byrne. Evidence is clear. Suffocation after a strong blow to the left-hand side of her jaw indicating possible right-handed attacker. It is believed the strike brought temporary incapacity, unconsciousness, thus allowing the plastic hood and strapping to be placed without hinderance from the victim. It was clearly premeditated. Medical evidence suggests no sexual motive. She did not appear to have recovered consciousness after the blow as there was no sign to remove the plastic. A further and full post-mortem will take place, and you will be updated.'

'Anything from Forensics?' DC Colin Drake asked. Colin had been around the block more than once, although he had not long been with the Merseyside force. However, he had soon settled in. 'Was the killer in the flat? Welcomed in? Known to the woman?'

His eager questions flowed.

'Good questions. Speaking with her neighbours, Caitlin was in the habit of leaving doors ajar when popping to the shops opposite, not only to her flat but also the front door to the building. She'd been confronted by a number of concerned residents. "I'm usually only a tick," was her normal excuse even though she'd been tackled on more than one occasion. From all accounts she did her own thing, and hers and the neighbours' security obviously weren't a concern. As I'm sure you're aware, the area has experienced its fair amount of antisocial behaviour and trouble, usually from young people. This is particularly evident in the local park area and by the main road shops opposite.'

'So, the killer might well have known about her disregard for security?' The statement hung in the air as a few heads nodded, not for long, as April quickly responded.

'It seems likely at this stage but usually I don't subscribe to coincidences.' She shook her head.

'DNA?'

'Indeed, we have Caitlin's and a number of other touch samples but as of yet, none is showing on the database, but it's early days. We always want tomorrow yesterday.'

Lucy came in and moved to the front. She spoke quietly to April and then handed her a small file before plugging a data stick into the interactive board. She found the icon, opened the file, nodding at April who addressed the group again.

'Apparently, an interesting fact from one of the earlier attacks by the same group, or at least some of them, has come to light. It shows the same pedestrian, The Controller, we believe him to be, and we'll know him from that title for general reference to save confusion.'

On screen appeared a short clip of the incident. Lucy paused it. 'This is just over three months ago. The shop you see trades in second hand goods – phones, guitars, cameras. It's where they exchange goods for cash. You can see The Controller to the right looking in the window of the shop next door.'

She ran on the CCTV. Two electric motorbikes appeared, one from the left, the other from the right. The passengers dismounted and struck the windows with hammers before grabbing items at random and stuffing them into bags. A third bike arrived, the passenger, although dismounted, remained facing out towards the road as if protecting the other two dismounted attackers. Pedestrians moved away quickly and those within the shop stayed inside, apart from one, a male, who, although moving out onto the pavement, removed his phone to capture the chaos. One of the attackers moved towards him. He quickly retreated inside but was either brave or foolish enough to keep on videoing the drama.

April had seen this before but only now did she see The Controller remove his phone and record the man.

Lucy continued. 'Digital forensics have tracked through social media posts for this date and discovered that this individual's footage was uploaded within a few minutes of the robbery ending. Evidence taken from this angle and the distance analysis suggests it can't have been taken by any other person.' She paused and looked at her colleagues. 'From that, they have identified the man.' An image appeared on screen accompanied by his details. 'His name is Ghulam Mohammed. He was one of many young men who we believe crossed the channel illegally last May and has been housed in various locations since that time. The last known temporary home is a house in Blackpool, a government rented house of multi-occupancy he shared with other young males awaiting asylum. However, his whereabouts have been unknown since late May. His phone stopped and there's been no communication since. As you're aware, many of these young men awaiting asylum can and do disappear into the black market, the criminal underworld, drawn by offers of work and a better life, particularly if they believe they do not stand any chance of getting asylum. Although there was some concern about his wellbeing, it was understood that was the reason he did not return.'

Colin coughed as if to put his idea forward. 'There's a report that suggests over a million people have entered the country over and above those we apprehend in small boats and lorries – shall we say – "undocumented"?' He paused. 'We've seen them walk up the beaches and meld into the scenery. Yes, "undocumented" is my polite label, one I've heard before on numerous occasions. They are brought in to work and probably become little more than disposable slave labour at the hands of the criminal fraternity. I'm old enough to remember the Morecambe cockling tragedy where twenty-one illegal Chinese were drowned when the tide came in. I was a fresh-faced copper in Lancashire when that hit the news. Who knows how many of the present-day "undocumented" folk fail to see another day? Remember though, they're all searching for some kind of freedom, whatever route they take and let's not forget the hardship they suffer.' Colin raised his eyebrows. There was a pause as his words sank in.

'What was his reason to be in the shop?' April asked. 'Do we know?'

'We're checking,' Lucy added. 'All we know about Ghulam Mohammed is that he's been on the missing list since that week. Social media posts, as well as the usual calls to the public, have proved fruitless. It's as if, like so many others, he's evaporated. We have no evidence to suggest there's a link to this present case but from what's recently been uncovered, and from the facts I see here, it cannot and will not be ruled out. I don't need to mention the statistics. In cases of people going missing for over a month, ninety percent never return. And if you look at the number in that sad category, he's one of thousands.'

'Considering the many other bike robberies, can we identify similarities to this case? Possible abduction, murder?' April quizzed.

'Not as far as we can see. Although they were present at each one, what I call "the hidden eyes", the nosey parkers, the video-recording individuals who immediately whip out their phones, but as yet, we haven't tracked their footage to social media. It's all about resources as you know. That doesn't mean to say the footage wasn't posted but those present might have closed down or changed their social media pages or ...' Colin failed to finish his train of thought as uncertainty overcame him. 'To be honest, April, it's all beyond me. What does frighten me are the unbeknown digital trails people leave in their wake, not even realising they do so. Much of this remains available for ever, somewhere within the multi-layered digital world, and some of the images are truly sickening.'

April pointed to the photograph of Ghulam Mohammed. 'The story of "Hansel and Gretel" comes immediately to mind. I want a revision, a new search for this chap. Get this image back out there. Someone who is now free but was unable to speak at the time might just be in a position to help. I know it's a long shot but from my experience ...'

'By any available means or method,' Skeeter announced cheekily, words that were close to her heart. In fact, they were tattooed on her torso in Latin; it was her charm, her amulet.

April nodded and smiled. 'Indeed, Skeeter, indeed.'

* * *

The weather had improved as the day lengthened. The sun had broken through the clouds and would surprise the west coast with its colourful and fiery retreat. The River Mersey always looked at its best at this time of day, if and when the cloud cover allowed. The river's normal, dreary, sludgy surface, a flat expanse at this point running between the Wirral and Liverpool proper, would miraculously change, fooling the trichromacy of the watchful eye into believing it held within its moving depths all the rich reds, oranges and shiny gold collected from all the treasure lost over the many years.

Leaning on one of the metal posts that ran along the river's edge, he let his mind drift like the passing water whilst contemplating the hundreds of padlocks attached to the lengths of looping chain fencing. A chuckle bubbled in his throat as he considered the many good intentions promised when the shackle was snapped permanently shut, locking one sincere heart full of promises to another. Cynically, as if to spoil the magic, he wondered how many of those romantic liaisons were now broken, some before they truly started, his own included. Considering the devastation the salty air had wrought on many of those locks made of mild steel, he believed it to be a substantial number. 'The river's edge is linked with good intentions … If only life were so simple,' he mused in a whisper that was quickly lost on the estuary breeze. He dug into his pocket to retrieve a handkerchief but immediately he felt the coarse fabric of the red hood; it was the very reason he was here. Turning, he checked the time on the Liver Building clock and headed towards the dock road. The late afternoon chill was already growing and the heat of the falling sun's ombré played tricks with the eye.

* * *

Crosby and the towering red cranes could not have come soon enough. It had been a long day and the walk along the dock road was tedious. As the edge of the land appeared, clear of buildings and obstacles, his eyes focused on the cut-like slice of blood red sky that now formed the only horizon way out to sea. It did not bleed for long, and within moments the end of the day had given way to darkness. However, soon he would be home. He yearned for the bottle, to be able to sit, contemplate and obliterate the memories that always came hand in glove with the shadows. He also realised there was hope, he was beginning to win, take his revenge and he knew, rightly or wrongly, he was emotionally stronger than he had been since those tragic days. After all, he had convinced himself that revenge, no matter how misguided, how much of an old wives' tale, drained the anger – squeezed the pus from the boil. How many deaths would it take before he could return to a normal life? He had no answer, but two had brought a whole new perspective and, in some ways, those deaths had shone light onto the uncertain pathway on which he had chosen to walk.

* * *

After kissing the silver-framed photograph as he did each evening when his demons allowed, he poured a glass from the bottle of whisky, held it to the light, popped his nose on the rim and closed his eyes before adding a single cube of ice. Moving the glass to his ear, he listened to its immediate cracking sounds of surrender, sounds not too dissimilar from the pleas of his two victims when the inevitable was suddenly realised. 'To a new day!' He took a sip. He studied the roll of red hessian material on the coffee table, the other materials and the glue, needle and threads. He had a new hood to make.

CHAPTER 16

DC Michael Peet removed his jacket from the back of his chair, slipped it on and stretched, before removing his bag from beneath his desk. Another night shift was finishing. The files on which he had worked had been logged with his usual degree of diligence. He had appreciated the note of thanks from April and was surprised there was no further request. The videos he had seen the previous evening had certainly sparked his interest and had taken him to the edge of a number of rabbit holes, but those areas of curiosity would have to wait, that is, apart from one. For some reason it had plagued his thoughts throughout the shift, it gnawed at him leaving no option but to investigate further in his own time.

* * *

The electric bikes had been charged and checked. The WhatsApp messages had been sent, finalising the details. Alan Green had followed the instructions to the letter. The nerves fluttered in his stomach more strongly than he had previously experienced, but he liked to be challenged. From his initial understanding of the task, carrying the necessary large, long-handled hammers had been a worry but Smigga had come up with the idea of using Velcro straps to attach them to the bikes, making the tool part of the frame. They would also be trapped by the legs of both rider and pillion for additional security. On arrival, they could be easily removed. It had been tested and according to its amateur designer, worked without affecting the balance of the bike. The bikes were originally designed to be road legal but then insurance and registration plates would be required. These had come from the dark market with scrubbed serial numbers, a ten-thousand watt peak motor that was good for sixty-five miles per hour two up, although the bikes were originally designed for one – that small problem had been easily rectified. This made them light in weight, incredibly quick off the mark and difficult to catch in towns where their manoeuvrability could outperform most other forms of transport.

Alan looked at his passenger and pushed his thumb up as they both pulled on the sweaters and hood combination. Each adjusted it to ensure a tight fit and clear visibility before he checked the time on his phone. They had a rendezvous point and instructions for their route to it. For much of that journey they would be away from the main roads, slipping down back alleys, streets and passageways. For one of the bikes, part of the route would be along the canal and then, once nearer the city centre, it was a case of keeping an eye open for, and whenever possible keeping away from, the police. If any rider felt compromised, they would abort. Three bikes not meeting at the set point would bring immediate cancellation. The passengers would communicate if problems occurred.

Sparra and pillion were the last to arrive as he slid the bike to a halt. The three riders gave a thumbs up. Alan checked the time. They were on schedule. Although only three bikes in total, they were like modern day riders of the apocalypse. They set off in turn, each fifteen seconds apart, bringing only what they believed to be a robbery to the set target, but they would, unbeknown to them, as they had done on two previous occasions, also bring to one person, a victim as yet unknown, a cruel demise.

* * *

Despite feeing weary, Michael Peet had grabbed a coffee and had gone straight to his study. The nag seemed to not only tumble in his stomach but also fill his mind, making rest impossible. His wife and kids were still in bed and would not rise for another hour. He had an itch to scratch. The computer screen depicted the character, a fictitious creation and something from his past that he had mulled over during his shift: Red Hood. He could not recall from where he had remembered the character, maybe the internet but more likely a comic but there he was, looking straight back at him. He read the back story, growing increasingly confused, yet at the same time, more intrigued. The link was with the DC comics, the Joker, Batman and his sidekick, Robin. The idea drew him in as he suspended his disbelief. For some time, he was so engrossed, he forgot momentarily the reason he had started the search.

Although the story fascinated him, he was quickly feeling that the rabbit hole in which he now found himself was growing deeper and probably would be, if truth be told, a pointless exercise. Sleep called. He jotted down key words about the story, 'Joker', 'chemicals', 'avenger', 'cruel', 'brutal' and then in block capitals, the words, 'RED HOOD'. He slid the keyboard towards the screen, folded his arms and leaned forward to rest his head. Within the hour, his wife woke him.

'Michael Peet just what are you doing? Bed. How long have you been propped up here?' There was concern in her voice.

He turned quickly. 'Sorry. I just needed—' He did not finish. Standing, he kissed her forehead. 'I love you, Mrs Peet.'

'Daddy!' The children ran and clung to his legs.

* * *

The roads by the river were busy. The steady flow of stop-start traffic made the ride worse by the number of lights and pedestrians interfering with the movement along The Strand. Once the route of the overhead railway, it was now one of the major arteries of the city that runs before the Three Graces, the magnificent buildings that are such an iconic part of the Liverpool waterfront. The constant traffic flow was also occasionally thrown into disarray by the wail of emergency vehicles. The flash of blue and the wail of sirens was a surefire way to break the day's routine.

The morning had dawned bright, and the aqueous sky appeared like a smudged colour wash, giving no hint of the day's weather. A solitary figure stood in the doorway on the corner of Whitechapel and Peter Street. His flat, cloth cap hung limply to either side of the face, covering the upper part of his ears, a modern-day fashion accessory born from an historical television series. He checked his watch for the third time before glancing back at St John's Beacon, the four-hundred-foot-high viewing platform that was once the home to Radio City. Its simple modernity seemed in total contrast to some of the buildings at its base. After leaving and turning right, it took him four minutes to enter the pedestrian area, and he needed to be another ninety metres further along the road for the set time. Pausing he looked back. On time, the three bikes sped past, all were in line, the first blazing the trail swerving and weaving avoiding stunned pedestrians. Their progress was silent and swift. The red-hooded riders bent forward, fully focused and quick. Some people simply ignored them casting only a glance before continuing, after all, this was a frequent occurrence in the city. Others jumped clear. Protesting voices echoed withing the confines of the roadway. He followed them at a gentle pace, knowing their destination. Within minutes and far too early, they were returning but he could see only two bikes, their progress erratic and eager. He then saw the commotion further up the road. A bike was down. A crowd had gathered.

Noting the location of the street's CCTV cameras, he positioned himself out of view but close to the other spectators. 'What's happened?' His strong accent caused a woman to turn.

She looked at the face partially hidden by the surgical mask. 'They were robbing the jewellers, bloody big hammers they had. Smashed the two windows whilst the bikes shot off down the road. They had red hoods and one of the dickheads faced the crowd, threatening like. He had like some kind of pointed sword. Anyroad up, when the bikes returned, two guys grabbed one of the gang members and decked him with a single punch. The others left what they carried, jumped on the bikes and scarpered quick like; the bastard is over there. He's been held down. The bike rider tried to frighten the bloke, but he managed to grab and smack the pillion before picking up one of the hammers and tossing it through the spokes of the bike's front wheel. The rider went arse over tit and hit the deck like a sack of shit. Excuse my French.' She turned and grinned. 'Sadly, unlike the first one, he managed to get up and run. Fucking parasites, good hiding is what they need. Never did us any harm.'

'Thanks, love.' He turned and watched the crowd as a siren broke above the bustle. He watched as a number of the spectators filmed the event. From those, he wondered who might be the one to post the action on social media – it could even be going out live as he watched. As far as he could see, there was only one of the gang still on the ground next to the downed bike. The second, the driver, had managed to make his escape as there was no commotion away from the immediate scene.

The police vehicle arrived on scene and the crowd opened allowing the car to get closer. Three police officers climbed out. To the observer, it was the pillion who was on the ground. He had been divested of the sweater and hood. Blood was gushing from his mouth and nose. A number of people continued to record the scene. Unbeknown to them, they, too, were being photographed.

April received the call. She noted the description of those involved. It was the same gang. Without hesitation, she contacted City Watch, requesting the live camera coverage. It was immediately patched through for the specific area. Communicating with the camera operator she requested it be zoomed on the main group who were now being moved back from the incident, leaving only two police officers and the one captive. She scanned the group looking for anyone wearing a face covering. As she gave directional instructions, she watched the screen as it panned from one side to the other. She failed to locate anyone who resembled The Controller.

'Is there a way of looking directly below the camera?' Her request seemed desperate and lacked confidence. She was swiftly informed that there was not. The man for whom she searched was, as far as she could see, not present.

CHAPTER 17

By late afternoon, each had seen the news before heading to the dragon cave.

'What the fuck happened?'

Alan Green's voice reverberated around the cavernous space, a familiar void that now seemed overly claustrophobic and cold, their presence insignificant. To those before him, it seemed more a courtroom that a place of sanctuary.

'The guy came out of nowhere and before Crabtree could do anything, he was on the deck.'

His protest was made difficult through his swollen lips, his voice was also markedly different. Sparra looked decidedly the worse for wear. The over-the-handlebars fall had resulted in damage to his right eye, nose and the loss of both front teeth; they appeared broken and jagged a few millimetres beneath the gum.

'Look at the fooking state!' He pointed to the damage.

If Green were honest, the damage looked far worse in the shadowy torchlight that constrained the colour spectrum to various shades of black and grey, contrasting sharply with the white of his skin. He rested a hand on his friend's shoulder. 'I saw your fall. I turned just as it happened. Fuck, you were lucky not once, but twice, for one you didn't break your neck, and secondly, you managed to run away.'

'Thanks! Small comfort, I guess? I take it you've seen the news?' Sparra looked at each face. 'We're it and from what I can see we're linked to some sort of murder.' His voice wobbled as he said the word before bringing it back under control. 'Fook, Greenie, I want bloody out. We're on national fooking telly for Christ's sake. CCTV footage. I could see my arse going over my fooking tits.'

'Your hoods were on TV, your faces were hidden and if you hadn't been wearing that then they couldn't show that face of yours now until after the watershed as you'd scare the bloody nippers.'

Green's quick and flippant reply was meant to defuse their anger, appease their uncertainty but it had the opposite effect and made Sparra stand. Smigga followed as if the move were rehearsed.

'You don't seem to be able to smell the shit we're in and from where I'm standing, it's up to our fooking necks.' Sparra's hand came towards his chin. 'We're in it up to here. Any road up, we've had a chat. Something's bloody not right, nobody gives something for nothin', my old man always said that. The guy, your guy. Who is he and what's he really after?'

Smigga broke in. 'You know Crabtree will spill the beans as soon as they say he's linked to some woman's murder. I know I would right after I'd shit myself. So, as Sparra says, what the fuck do you know? What are you not telling us? Who's this dangerous wanker with the cash ... this "Bossman"?'

For once, Green had no answer. He remained seated. His inability to speak seemed to last for ever and the resulting silence hovered and lingered like a bad smell as his growing anger festered. Rubbing his face, more out of desperation than to glean inspiration, his headlight searched his friends' faces in turn.

'I'm as much in the dark as you men. He just rang me, challenged me out of the blue. It just seemed too good an opportunity to turn down. I didn't ask.' Only now did Green begin to question himself, ask the obvious questions, and a hot flush of guilt seeped through his body.

'Fook off!' For the one word, his favourite word, the vowels were overly exaggerated owing to the damage to his mouth. It not only highlighted Sparra's accent but reinforced his anger. 'If you've not noticed, we're not in the fooking dark, you've got a fooking headlamp and it's not giving us a clear understanding of why. You're supposed to be our leader and therefore in fooking control. We trusted you, Crabby trusted you. What are we going to do? More to the point, Greenie, what are you going to do?'

Green stood. He was a few inches taller than either man. He leaned towards them.

'Funny how you men never refuse the cash and neither do you refuse the fun, but you, Sparra, you get jelly legs when something out of our control happens. You wobble,' he mimicked, his legs shaking, the beam of his lamp dancing on the roughly hewn walls. 'You're like Grobbellar when he was facing penalties. You're shitbags the pair of you. You speak for the others, do you?' Greenie let his headlamp now rest on Smigga's face, making him look away. 'The answer to that is "no". Some are loyal, remain loyal when the shit gets to there.' He moved his hand swiftly to his chin. 'They will follow through thick, and as you would say, fooking thin.' He paused, his anger growing. 'What should we do? I'll tell you what to do. Strip your bike Smigga and get it in here. Mine's already here. I take it you came here on it? Strip it and get it in. Sparra can help you as he's lost his.' The words hung as heavily as their now increasing guilt. 'Spread the parts around this place. Hide them by covering them with rocks. Use your brains. Everything gets stashed here and I mean everything. Hoods, clothing, the lot.'

'And when the Bizzies knock, then what?' Smigga goaded. 'They'll come, as they'll grab Crabby's phone, search every call, collect and check his saved numbers. Knowing his crap memory, he'll not have deleted them. What then?'

'What fooking then, Greenie? If they come for me, they come for us all, that I can promise.' As Sparra spoke he moved back uncertain as to Green's reaction.

'You don't meet again. You leave your business phones in here, too, and only you will know where you've stashed them, and then you fuck off out of my sight. Afterwards, this place becomes out of bounds. That, boys, is not a warning, it's a fooking threat,' he mimicked. 'Nobody compromises this place, my place. Got it?'

There was an immediate silence, hanging heavily as the dark air. 'Got it.' They spoke in unison. As they turned to leave, the lights they carried bounced off the stone walls and columns.

'Hey Smigga, who the fook's this Grobbellar bloke he was talking about?'

'It's Green. He makes stuff up. Just ignore him.'

* * *

Within an hour of reaching the custody suite, the doctor had inspected and treated the damage to Graham Crabtree's face in the presence of a duty solicitor. One of the blows had split the left eyebrow and butterfly sutures had been applied. The intensity of the further struggle and the resulting blows had brought a number of contusions that had coloured his face the various shades normally found in an evening storm cloud. His thunderous protestations were not too dissimilar; now, however, when the realisation of his predicament had dawned, he cut a forlorn and fragile figure as he waited in the holding cell of Copy Lane Station.

After the necessary risk assessment had been completed, it was felt appropriate for his own welfare that his clothes be removed, and he be dressed in anti-rip clothing. The swift procedure had consolidated the severity of the situation in which he found himself and the more that process continued, the more his anxiety and uncertainty became clear. The two members of the public responsible for his injuries had been released once their statements had been taken, however, the CCTV footage was clear to see.

As Skeeter and Tony entered the interview room, the custody officer moved back towards the door. She sat and Tony remained standing. Skeeter smiled at the duty solicitor before reminding Crabtree that he had been cautioned and charged. Aggravated robbery was a serious offence, but evidence suggested that a more sinister crime had been committed. Crabtree briefly regarded the man next to him and then Skeeter, before lowering his head as she read out loud from the sheet before her. It was his personal details. He was known to the police; his youth record was extensive.

'Good with a needle and thread, Mr Crabtree?' She watched as his hand touched his eyebrow. She smiled inwardly before taking the bagged hooded sweater he had been wearing, placed it on the table before him and patted it. 'A collage of patches and stitches. Creative, you're quite the tailor.' She waited but there was no response. 'Here you are, too, the pillion on a motorcycle on one of your, shall we say, better, more successful days.' She put the photograph on top of the hood. 'This was your daring raid on the electronics' shop. The first time you had two faces and, as you can see, identical tailoring to this we have here.'

Crabtree looked at the photograph taken from Caitlin's phone. Only then did he look directly at Skeeter.

'Are you a bloke in drag or just a fucking ugly woman? And if you must know, no, that's not me.'

The solicitor sat back and raised one eyebrow. It was clear his advice had been ignored. The insult flew over Skeeter's head. Even though it was creative of sorts, she had heard worse.

'So, this isn't yours or this isn't you?' He shook his head. 'It was removed from you at the scene of the incident, but it doesn't belong to you? I believe your DNA will be all over it, Mr Crabtree.'

'I need a piss. You can't deny me a piss.'

Skeeter turned to the custody officer who approached him adding a metal cuff to his left wrist. 'He'll take you. I'll be here when you return.' She smiled as a second officer entered. 'He'll be going, too, Mr Crabtree. Neither is in drag and, I assure you, neither is a woman.'

'Fuck you.'

'Mr Crabtree.' She waited for him to pause. 'Don't forget to wash your hands.'

The duty solicitor coughed to conceal his amusement.

Expert hands tied the half Windsor knot in the striped, silk tie, the procedure made easier by checking in the mirror that was positioned above the fireplace. Once satisfied with the result, he glanced at the face trapped behind the glass, the silver frame reflecting the light. His heart sank momentarily but then the scrap of paper on the coffee table, the personal details of the next victim, provided an immediate fillip.

'Nearly there.'

His smile was sincere. He, however, could wait, there was no rush as now work called. Four days were expected and soon it would be five. The staggered return had been beneficial. Light duties, they had said, and they had been right, but for the wrong reasons. He checked his watch. He needed to dash.

* * *

The interview had proved tedious. It was decided to hold him in custody overnight.

Back in the Incident Room, Skeeter watched, again, as the video started. She felt that from the little she had seen of him he could not be involved in a murder. Crabtree was part of the game, but it was clear he was not bright enough to be the leader. She was sure he could only follow. He was a foot soldier, unquestioning and obedient but she felt he knew his limits. She had interviewed enough yobs, people who would never make a success in life, those who had been manipulated and controlled all their lives and he was one. Once digital forensics had found his call history, his contacts, they would soon know the others involved and with that, they should discover if there were, as they believed to be the case, a controller.

Crabtree could sweat a little longer.

CHAPTER 18

Professional photographer Paul Burrows watched the screen on the control pad as he flew the drone down the Crosby coast. The day's light and cloud pattern contrived to create perfect conditions for the purpose of capturing video footage of the iron men, the Anthony Gormley figures, positioned within the expanse of sands. Each figure was separated by some distance, deliberately to allow some to remain within the bounds of the Liverpool waters. Others stood proudly nearer to the land where the sand had been whipped from beneath their feet, leaving them literally high and dry on their metal foundations.

Most were salt-weathered and worn, each had taken on its own patina and personality. Some figures had been altered, helped along the way with paint, feathers and various pieces of flotsam and jetsam added through creative human interaction.

Flying over the tide, the drone's 4K Hasselblad camera picked out Seaforth's giraffe-like cranes, soldier straight and motionless and, for Paul Burrows, they were a favourite shot. The drone turned, a sweeping, professional approach taking each figure in turn, flying towards each face and keeping as low as possible whilst skimming the water's surface. It was difficult to comprehend how each could be so different as they had all been identical when they were placed there in 2007. It was the differences, the varied colours and disfiguring erosion, which made them targets for so many photographers.

The drone's flight had been heard and watched by another spectator; it was not always easy to spot, particularly when flying at low level or when in hover mode. However, the pilot, leaning on the promenade railing, controller in hand, was clear to see. He never looked up, his eyes remaining on the screen before him. The stranger moved closer until he was practically on the pilot's shoulder.

'Technology these days. It's so clever. Hobby, is it?' The stranger's voice was gentle but had a rich Scouse accent as he deliberately scanned towards the sea's edge as if looking for the drone.

Initially, the pilot did not speak. He moved his hand from one of the controls towards his pocket and pulled out a business card, quickly offering it to the stranger before going back to the controls.

'Professional, Paul Burrow's Photography. You'll be able to see this on my YouTube page. It's called, The Scouser's Eye. Proving popular, too, particularly when the big cruise ships come in. Got some great footage of the *Prince of Wales* the other week. Been one of my best sellers.' He turned briefly towards the stranger. 'That's an aircraft carrier by the way.'

The stranger looked at the card and then for the drone. 'Yes, saw it on the news. Cheers, like. I'll take a look at your site.'

Watching the drone approach one of the iron men, one that was only too familiar, he quickly moved away.

It was as Burrows approached this, the eighth figure to be visited, that he saw it and it was certainly not what he had expected. He brought the drone to a hover. The crude, contrasting facial features on the bedraggled, red hood stared back at the camera. He quickly realised he had seen the like of it before, or one very similar. With some urgency, he brought the drone home. He had been shocked by his discovery and needed to inform the police.

The stranger observed the man's change in body posture. He could see the urgency, the controlled panic as the drone returned. It raised a smile.

CHAPTER 19

April studied the image she held, as a video played on the interactive screen. The camera shots from the drone were clear as it zoomed in flying low over the grey water. A tidal marker passed to the right, a weather-beaten metal triangle on what looked like a vertical steel girder; most of the paint had disappeared, a victim of the incessant daily salt sprays, and barnacles had coated much of the structure. This was the second running of the video for April, and she concentrated closely on the next section as the drone approached one of the metal men. It was clear from the sudden stop that the pilot's focus and curiosity was on the sculpture's alien red head covering, a hood, a red hood that sagged over either shoulder through saturation by rain or immersion in sea water. It covered the head of the metal man completely, whilst sea water lapped the figure's brown and rust flaked torso, much of which was now deformed by barnacles and salt corrosion. The drone's rotating blades whipped the water's surface into a frenzy as it hovered at a static, safe distance but the camera stared and surveyed the collaged, patchwork face. Even though the hood sagged heavily, the drooping facial features were still familiar and recognisable. April paused the video.

Next to the screen was a coastal map locating and numbering the exact position of the one hundred life size metal figures dotted along the stretch of the Crosby coast. This one figure had been circled for identification.

Skeeter stood to her right, leaned closer to the screen and checked a photograph she held. 'There's a cable tie round the neck. It's visible there beneath that fold.' She rested her finger on the screen.

'We have a team attending. It's been decided to wait until the water level falls before a full inspection is made. Although it's unlikely any forensic evidence will be discovered we can always hope. We also have the Crosby Coastguard Rescue Team there. The sands can be tricky, especially after the tide has receded.'

'The video?' Skeeter asked as she looked more closely at the map.

'Sent in by a member of the public, a regular drone pilot, professional photographer. Posts a lot on social media on his YouTube page, 'The Scouser's Eye'. You've probably seen his stuff, mainly shot around the Pier Head. Thankfully for us, he'd seen the news about the bike robberies and the hoods worn. He called immediately and we requested he send the video through. We've also asked for discretion and that the footage should not be published. I've also restricted the information as I don't want it leaking to the press or public as yet.'

'Time?' Skeeter asked.

She had a suspicion the hood could be a red herring, some crank playing games after the public release of the close-up shots of the head gear taken from CCTV of the robbery but then thought better of it; for one thing, the time-scale would not fit. Besides, it would have to have been placed on the figure during the last low tide.

'Approximately an hour ago. I know what you're thinking, low tide is expected within the hour. I also checked the time between high tides. Twelve hours give or take so from low to high is six. This could have been placed on the night Caitlin died or within the next change of tides.'

'Why?' Skeeter asked as she mulled over the whole idea. 'Why not just bag it, weight it and toss it into the river at any point, like everything that's known to man and God that's been used in a crime. That way it would never be found. Why the performance?'

'I have a horrible feeling this could be part of a game. If our belief is correct, that Ghulam Mohammed was killed, murdered by the same person, his death went unnoticed. There was limited press coverage and if you're trying to be noticed, make a statement, that's not desirable. A certain type of killer needs to thrust their actions into the public eye; they plan an elaborate game, a sinister game like chess where people become the pieces, a game of chance where they know they can win but also lose.'

'So did they miss something, some clue with Ghulam?'

'It's possible. It's also probable not much effort went into the investigation.'

* * *

Alan Green's phone rang twice and then stopped. Knowing the caller, he held his phone momentarily as anger spread across his face. It rang again. He took the call but only listened.

'Your boys were not what you said they were, Mr Green. You said they could work to order, to definitive instructions. They were a shambles and totally out of their depth, but you know that. One of them is now with our constabulary, the Bizzies. You, however, were excellent. I saw the confidence you demonstrated, the accuracy of your riding and it did not go unnoticed. Your action to distract the crowd as you tried to assist your fallen man to give him time to stand and run was impressive. So, what now?' He paused briefly knowing Green would fail to answer. 'There's nothing for the others I'm afraid but for you, should you wish, I have plans. No more sharing the money, it will be for you and you alone.' There was another pause. Green looked round in the hope of spotting the caller. 'You will not see me even though I can clearly see you. I feel sure the Bizzies will be paying you a visit. You know that and you have time to plan for it, or, if you are uncomfortable with that, you could bugger off, go into hiding. I'll be in touch, and we'll work together again if that's what you'd like. It will be difficult and a true challenge. If you agree, stand by Captain "Johnnie" Walker's statue on the Pier Head at seven-thirty tonight. It's the statue of the man with the binoculars. If you're there, Greenie, then we shall … if you're not there then you're alone. This phone, like yours, is a throwaway and if you're not there … Remember, Mr Green, everyone needs a captain, even you, so think carefully about your next decision and your future steps. Your friends will sell you down the river to save their skins. They're scallies.'

The call ended. The Bossman always seemed to communicate in riddles, but the false Scouse accent seemed even stronger than ever. He had never seen him, but he felt sure he did not like him. For the first time since receiving the call, he realised he had not uttered a word.

* * *

April took the call as she reflected on the report detailing the interview with Crabtree. It was Michael Peet. She checked her watch. He was not due in for another two hours.

'Kids keeping you up?' She laughed. 'You're the last person I expected to hear from at this time.'

'Something's been nagging me. I did some overtime at home when I got in. What do you know about a character by the name of Red Hood?'

'You'll not be aware, but we've discovered a red hood that's not dissimilar to those worn by the riders, those videoed by Caitlin Byrnes who was subsequently murdered. This one is very close in design, construction and detail but it's not a match for any seen on her footage or the CCTV we hold. It was found covering the head of one of the Gormley statues and one that's only accessible at low tide; that fact might be crucial as chronological evidence. You'll see the details and the video we received when you come in tonight. Sorry, I digress but to answer your question, Michael. Red Hood? … nothing.'

'April, Red Hood is a comic book character.' He paused as if suddenly lacking in conviction. 'Please don't think me stupid but there's a fascinating back story to the character. Jason Todd was one of the original Robins, you know, Batman's sidekick. He was adopted by Batman, who became his surrogate father, but he was killed by The Joker. Anyway, to cut a long story short, Robin returned from the grave and, realising Batman hadn't avenged his death, he found The Joker and brutally beat him taking his red hood outfit. As far as I can make out, he, The Joker, was originally known as, The Red Hood, and he formed the Red Hood Gang—'

April broke in. 'Michael, have you been drinking?'

Michael laughed. 'I knew you'd say that. Do me a small favour and, when time permits, look at the back story of Red Hood and Jason Todd. Hopefully you'll quickly see the connections and therefore you might understand that the thalamus in my brain is not playing tricks on me!' He chuckled as if embarrassed. 'Be warned, it's quite a rabbit hole. I've emailed you some links so you've no excuse.' She heard the cry of a child in the background. 'Sorry, I must go.'

'Michael. Your thalamus?' It was too late, he had already hung up.

Realising she had been given some homework, April jotted down some notes. Michael's hunches had often turned out to be very fruitful and even though this one bordered on the bizarre, she knew she would have to investigate. She then googled the word 'thalamus' and discovered it to be the part of the brain that was crucial in controlling imagination, consciousness and abstract thought.

* * *

Removing the notes from his pocket, he slipped them onto the table. He undid his tie and opened the top button of his shirt. The afternoon in the office, his half day, had passed more quickly than he had hoped; he had been busy as there had been much to catch up on. Colleagues had continued to show him kindness and were clearly sensitive and caring. It surprised him after such a length of time had passed since the fateful day. He thought there would be a growing degree of resentment for the amount of compassionate leave he had received and the additional workload they had shared, after all, he had no physical scars and there appeared to be no lasting emotional ones now visible.

The Facebook post of the attack on the jeweller's shop had appeared within minutes and had been shared extensively. The scourge of the bike gangs had been on the local and national news and, in particular, this one owing to the red head coverings. It was the first time the moniker, The Red Hood Gang, had been attached in a news bulletin. It had made him smile. Seeing the reporter at the location brought a frisson of excitement and even more so as he watched the interview with the police offi-cer. He was getting there. He raised his glass to the screen. 'The Red Hood Gang. They are no more.' He took a sip from the glass. 'But there may well be a Joker still in the pack.'

He stood. He had work to do.

The name Carl Jenkins was scribbled on the first piece of paper. The subsequent scripts held a collection of personal details removed from Carl's various social media posts. Through careful deduction, a face had emerged from a number of those posts, matching the photographs he had taken at the scene of the robbery. It had not taken long to find the real Carl Jenkins, to discover his address as well as his occupation. The digital world was convenient, but it was also informative and therefore potentially dangerous. It opened up the unwary and the careless to unforeseen dangers and highlighted their vulnerability. It informed of personal, daily habits. It was this information he found so vital.

Checking his watch, he collected the papers and added the address of a specific location into Google maps. He decided on the best route he should take to arrive and, also an alternative to exit as safely and discreetly as possible.

CHAPTER 20

April had walked Tico along the beach and enjoyed the sunset; the haunting gulls' calls and the tumbling waves had formed the accompanying soundtrack. Those swift, dying moments, watching the sea swallow the glowing ball before spreading a palette of washed and diluted colours along the horizon, were ones to savour. It always amazed her the way aquamarine and turquoise seemed to grow more present during the last gasps of the death of the day. She made mental notes for reference for selecting the colours for her stained glass windows. Breathing deeply, she enjoyed the fresh, sea air and felt invigorated.

The email had been waiting on her return home:

April,

The news reports on the socials have now referred to the bikers as, The Red Hood Gang, and there is a link to our own press release of the incident. I believe this will stick, so be aware, there may soon be copycat ride-by attacks.

Done your homework yet?

Michael

She was all too aware of the knock-on effects of the creation of a moniker for villains, whether they be individuals or gangs, but she was also a realist and knew this irresponsibility was often the work of either the press or the public. There was nothing they could do but to roll with it.

* * *

Alan Green stood in the gardens of Liverpool Parish Church of Our Lady and St Nicholas. The Liver Building stood before him like a huge iced cake as the many coloured lights illuminated its façade. He had never really taken time to study it but now, as it morphed from red to green, it held his full attention. The two huge metal birds perched on the tops of the clock towers gave it both a sinister and gothic appearance, which contrasted with the sky's pall, the darkening colours of dusk. His attention flicked to the clocks on both the church and the Liver Building, one seemed to be faster than the other. *All things considered, God's clock would probably be the correct time,* he mused. A new thought surfaced. *If God knew of my past, it might be set to deliberately tell the wrong time when being read by this sinner.* He chuckled at the very thought as he kicked an empty can and watched it disappear down the steps leading to the main road. The clatter reverberated within the confines of the grounds. The time, he believed, was 19.10. He had loads of time to locate the statue of the captain.

The traffic on The Strand was busy, but he knew from experience it had more than its share of pedestrian crossing places. He was soon over and walking down Water Street. The stiff breeze from the river brought a chill so he fastened his jacket before crossing Canada Boulevard. He spotted a statue across to his left but knew it was not the captain but the four musicians his grandfather had loved The Beatles. He took a moment to walk between them. His mind flicked to his grandad, the only man with whom he had ever formed a warm attachment. He could never remember him going out to work. He had supported Everton, a life-long blue. He always had a fag between his lips, and on many occasions, he would let Alan light one and take a crafty drag. 'Clear your lungs, it will. You mark my words.' Alan spoke the words he had heard so often as he then inhaled from the e-cig. The tune to 'Penny Lane' immediately came to mind, the high pitch trumpet and the melody put a skip in his step as he spotted the captain by the river's edge. Glancing up at the clock, he had three minutes.

Within the hour, April had descended into the threatened rabbit hole, and it helped her to understand some of the logic behind Michael's thinking. The main theme of the comic's early story was built on the premise of betrayed trust, revenge, avenging a wrong. There was clearly confusion as the avenger was seen to be taking the mantle of both hero and anti-hero, the good and the bad. The man that was once Batman's surrogate son and partner had been brought back to life and had stolen the red hood from the one who had killed him, The Joker, in the misguided belief he held all of the facts, that he knew the truth, but then much of that was an assumption borne only through his anger.

April sat back and sipped her red wine. 'Was The Controller, the mystery man we've seen on the CCTV footage, acting out of revenge, avenging a wrong from the past?' she asked Tico and his ears twitched. 'If so, what was the wrong? Could he be the killer of the woman who had videoed the robbery? Was he putting wrongs right in some misguided way? Was that why he left the red hood? Was it a signpost?' She jotted the word 'video' in capitals and underlined it twice. 'What truths did it hold, or were they half-truths, and if so, were they legitimate?'

In her career, she had seen much of that, where lack of knowledge of the facts, uncertainty of the truth, had devastated innocent lives. She had witnessed how people are quick to make judgements, seek incorrect retribution and how hatred can quickly be stoked. She was also experienced enough to know that facts were all that would count in successfully solving the murder and this speculative navel gazing could detract from the route they should take. She emptied her glass, jotted down a text message and sent it through to Michael's mobile:

Michael,

I've been down a certain rabbit hole. Fascinating!

Please check credit and debit card spending of Caitlin Byrnes and find the pub in which she had been drinking on the lunchtime of her death. Check CCTV for the man who supposedly chatted her up!!!! ASAP if possible.

* * *

Alan Green's phone rang. He waited. It stopped, but his heart raced as he looked around searching for anyone who might be The Controller. The whole Plaza was busy. He turned to the statue and struggled to read the inscription: Captain F J Walker

CB DSO***. He allowed his hand to touch the three stars out of curiosity. The phone rang again.

'Mr Green, good evening. Thank you for coming. I did so want you to be here. We do make a good team. I am surprised the Bizzies haven't been to see you, so we must continue to believe your friends are remaining just that and keeping their mouths shut. I have one more job for which we need neither bikes nor any of the others. You just need your hood and courage and even though this challenge may seem simple, it will take daring. There will be a large sum of cash for you, and you alone, should you accept.'

'Who are you and …' he paused, uncertain if he should continue. 'Did you kill the woman?'

He heard a deep laugh, it was high, almost feminine. 'Now why would I want to hurt anyone, let alone kill someone? Did I not always say, no weapons when we carried out our small raids?'

It was true. *Nobody should get hurt*. He remembered the conversation clearly and that had always been emphasised. Things just did not seem right.

'Should you wish to continue then the envelope containing a small part of your fee, and your instructions is in the capstan, you know it's location.'

As Alan looked at the captain, he visualised the capstan and its location. 'What the fuck! Why bring me here when I could be at the place I normally wait,' he grumbled.

'A lesson. The statue before you honours a very brave man. A sailor, a very successful hunter of submarines, a master tactician who could find the hidden and expose them so that he could destroy them before they could destroy him. What is to me fascinating, Mr Green, is that his son was killed in a British submarine during the war. His son.' There was a pause. 'And yet he continued his own battles, either through duty or revenge to destroy as many of the enemy as he could. A brave man, would you not agree?'

Green had stopped listening after the word tactician and watched as a ship passed in the centre of the river, its many lights reflecting on the river's black surface. If he were honest, he had had enough.

'Are you there?'

'How much?'

'Sorry, you seemed to have little or no interest. There is £1,000 in the envelope and a further four will come your way on completion.' He watched as Green started to walk towards the Albert Dock. 'If you are unhappy after reading what is needed from you, you can walk away and keep the money. I cannot be fairer than that.'

'Yes. Done.' As he spoke the phone seemed to go dead. 'Hello?' There was nothing. Slipping his phone away into his jacket he picked up speed, eager to see if it were true.

Sitting on the capstan he opened the envelope. Trapped within a plastic bag was the money, alongside the usual instructions. He needed some light and time to read them.

CHAPTER 21

Carl Jenkins's day began as always with a run through the dawn dim streets. Neither the weather nor the season was ever a consideration and, although not a naturally gifted runner, he was enthusiastic, consistent and determined. A health shock in his late twenties had been the wake-up call he had needed to change his ways. A relationship breakdown, late nights, beer and junk food had brought an uncomfortable increase in his blood pressure as well as to his waistline. That lifestyle, however, was in the past. He now followed his doctor's advice. The steady three miles each day, apart from Sunday and bank holidays, had become a ritual by which you could almost set a clock. The time, the route and the distance were, in his mind at least, his salvation.

Walking down Aigburth Drive after parking the car some distance away, the entrance to Sefton Park was clear, so, too, the stone obelisk. It stood semi-silhouetted against an artificially toned sky, cast by the city's many lights. It had always been there, and its reason, other than a welcome marker, was, to the observer, unknown. It was always a key part of Carl's daily run, too. It was his welcome turning point where he would pause and take a drink before heading back along the long, straight path through the park and home. The lights along that path still shone within their Victorian, iron standards.

On cue, the solitary figure ran centrally along the tarmac path, his pace neither laboured nor energetic. It was steady, much like everything else about Carl Jenkins's regime. As he approached the obelisk, he could see no one but that was not unusual. That was, however, soon to change.

* * *

Michael Peet had received April's text early in his shift. He had been successful in tracking Caitlin's credit card payments for the last month. He had also tracked the pub she had visited on the day she had lost her job. CCTV of the immediate vicinity had been requested, and an early visit had been organised for the next morning to check the footage from the cameras within the bar areas. Finding the man was a step closer to finding the killer.

* * *

The solitary figure leaning against the cold stone could now hear the plodding feet as they slowed, approaching the turning point before coming to a sudden standstill. The breathing was deep and heavy, broken only by the sound of a nostril being cleared with a swift snort. Moving away, he watched as Jenkins took a drink from a small bottle that seemed moulded to his hand; his head was back. There was a definite sheen of sweat to his face and much of his upper shirt was stained, dark and wet. It was the sign. Checking through three hundred and sixty degrees the only person visible was Jenkins.

'Mr Jenkins? Carl?' The words were barely audible, but Carl

turned immediately. The red hood staring back made him pause as if to refocus, to clear his eyes of the apparition standing before him.

'Fuck me!'

His words came as an explosion as he stepped backwards, droplets of water exploding from his mouth. Even as Carl staggered, the swiftly rising gloved fist still managed to catch him squarely on the chin exploiting his rear movement to the full. Carl's body fell, his head striking the stone base edge of the obelisk with a dull thud. Within seconds the clear plastic bag was pulled over his head and the electrician's tie secured. The same cloudy condensation appeared around the inner surface. Carl's closed eyes fluttered as blood pooled from the back of his head, thick and red forming what looked like a trapped, crimson cushion.

'We all learn lessons, Carl, but sometimes those lessons are learned too late.'

The hooded figure paused on his haunches, watching as the transparency on the surface of the bag was lost.

Saddened he could not explain the reason for the lesson, a lesson he had voiced to his two previous victims, he apologised as he slipped a red hood over the bag, different from the one he was wearing. That, too, was secured by another tie. He checked the immediate vicinity. A cyclist and a dog walker were now within view, still some distance away. Glancing at the words inscribed above the obsolete drinking fountain on the monument brought a quizzical look: 'Whosoever drinketh of the water shall thirst again. But whosoever drinketh of the water that I shall give them shall never thirst.'

After a swift glance at the area to ensure he had left nothing, he removed his own hood, stuffed it into his pocket, turned and ran towards the road and his car. Within forty-five minutes his own morning run would end along the sea front at Crosby. He knew the circumstances of the last hour would have helped him heal a little more. 'Can revenge be slaked like thirst? Can killing heal the broken?' The words were but a whisper lost to the breeze. Only time would tell. Staring out across the quicksilver surface of water, he suddenly felt energised.

* * *

April had arrived at her office early having a court case to attend at ten. She checked the time on her computer as she logged on. It was just before seven. She was so early she had only walked Tico for ten minutes, but he seemed more than happy to return to the warmth of the kitchen and the Aga.

Before April could settle, DC Phil Lipson entered. 'Didn't expect you in so early but I'm glad you are. We have three of the gang in custody, an early morning sweep when they were still in their pits. Always a good time. All linked to Graham Crabtree's phone. The good news for us, boss, one seems different from the others, timid like. You might even say, shit scared, if I were to be blunt. He doesn't have previous so the drawbridge he's raised is, shall we say, paper thin. All have been cautioned.' With a broad smile, Phil waved some paperwork.

April, allowing the chair to swing from side to side, gave the news some thought. 'He's a pillion or driver?'

What difference the answer to that question made was lost on Phil, but he had assumed him to be a pillion.

'He's younger than the others – seventeen, tall, though. His physique fits the description of one we've seen on the vids. No faces as you know. His name's John Rathbone, and, as I said, no previous, unlike the others. Graham Crabtree, Matthew Smith and Mick Webster. Mick insists we refer to him as Micky.' Phil raised his eyebrows. 'We've kept them separate. Thought we'd make them sweat a little as they know the others are here. They'll wonder just what's being revealed.'

April smiled. 'I want DC Colin Drake to interview all three. He's been round the block. He's shrewd, too, and up to speed on the case. With Rathbone, however, I want Kasum in there with him. Mother figure. You know the game. Colin goes hard and pops out of the room leaving Kasum to mop up any tears or hold back the floodgates.'

The more Phil got to know April, the more he admired her. He had been unsure when she had arrived, being a fast track academic, and female to boot. He had never believed in positive discrimination when it came to promotion within the force, but she had always been firm and fair when he had tested the waters and crossed the line. He raised a hand respectfully to his forehead and smiled.

He had only just left when April's mobile rang. She sighed, her best made plan of an early start was quickly crumbling. It was Skeeter.

'We have another body.' She paused, allowing the news to settle.

'Shit! Where?'

'This time they're wearing a red hood. Discovered at the base of the obelisk, Sefton Park, about fifteen minutes ago by a guy on a bike; a push bike, I'm pleased to say.'

April checked the time again. It was just after a quarter past seven. 'Bodies are usually found by joggers or dog walkers.'

'Indeed. I'm on my way there. Emergency services were called. I believe the guy who found him thought at first that he was a rough sleeper then realised the victim was in jogging gear. Rang 999 immediately and covered the body with his coat. He was afraid kids might see it. CSIs and paramedics should be arriving at any time. I'll be there in five minutes.'

'Report as soon as you've assessed the situation. Ensure

procedures are followed as temporary SIO.' She heard Skeeter call to someone close by. There was a moment's silence.

'Will do,' Skeeter mumbled, obviously distracted.

April dropped her phone onto the desk and took a deep breath, wondering what the third thing might be that morning as hurdles usually arrive in threes. Seconds later she received a text. It was from Michael confirming he had been successful in chasing Caitlin's card details, and he had arranged for Tony to visit the pub she had visited.

'They always come in threes,' she said, feeling as though now she might be able to fulfil the tasks she had come in early to complete.

CHAPTER 22

Of the four police cars present, one blocked the entry to the park and another police vehicle was positioned to the far side of the obelisk. The flashing blue strobes, bright and vivid in the low light of early morning, filled the area. The ambulance and the first responder's fast vehicle were also within the park grounds. Skeeter held up her ID and progressed towards the granite column with a degree of eagerness. The crime scene was in the process of being secured. The position of the body made that process difficult owing to the open aspect and the number of pedestrian and cycle routes converging on the obelisk.

A temporary screen had been erected to shield the body. It made Skeeter wonder if this had been a chance encounter, an opportunistic killing. The fact it followed all the signs of the last murder caused her to quickly dismiss her own nagging thoughts. Whoever did it was either well-organised and knew the victim's routine or was just plain lucky. Officers were now standing on the pathways directing the public away from the scene; at this time of day, the majority were dog walkers, joggers and cyclists.

A sergeant approached. Skeeter turned to face him. 'DS Warlock. I'm assuming the role of SIO until further notice.'

'Phil Campion. I was first on the scene. Secured it as best I could and started the scene log.' He removed his notebook and jotted down her name and time and checked his body cam was on. 'Paramedics in and CSIs on their way. Risk assessment done and the area has been secured to the best …' He did not need to state the obvious. His organisational skill seemed to come with ease. She touched his arm.

'Cheers.' She allowed herself a short but sincere smile. 'I can see we're in safe hands.'

The first responder and one other paramedic were standing close to the body, a number of foil blankets covered it even though the public, few as they were, were now well away and the temporary screen prevented viewing from the park entrance. Skeeter moved towards the group.

'DS Warlock, acting SIO.'

There was a moment's silence as the first responder rose to his feet.

'Chris Mott. As of fifteen minutes ago, I pronounced the victim dead. There was no pulse, clearly apnoea and asystole on two leads of the ECG. We couldn't check pupils, and we worked whilst trying to preserve the original position of the body as much as possible. Other than what I've described, nothing has been disturbed, and you'll understand why CPR was not attempted.' He dropped to one knee and lifted back the foil revealing the red hood. 'There's a tightly secured poly bag beneath that.' He raised an eyebrow. 'What vital evidence they may hold only you can guess. As you know, I can't give a time of death. Suffice to say we're not talking hours. I take it a doctor's been called?'

Skeeter squatted and looked carefully at the victim's head and shoulders.

The paramedic returned the foil with a degree of reverence. 'What the hell's the hood about?'

Skeeter looked around instinctively before leaning closer to Mott. 'Between you and me, this is the second.' She mimicked the hood by drawing her hands next to her head. 'Thought the news would've spread within your department as it's certainly bizarre and out of the ordinary.' She could see from his facial expression she was wrong.

'I heard about the murder. A young woman? Don't recall the hood being mentioned.'

'Not on the victim at the time, only a plastic bag and a tie but one was found later.'

Chris frowned. 'It was certainly not what I was expecting to see if I'm honest with you.' He quickly offered a puzzled look. 'Haven't there been similar hoods, worn during the bike robberies? Is there a connection?'

Skeeter raised her shoulders. 'Strong coincidence and I don't believe in those.'

He chuckled. 'When I saw it, it brought back a specific time in my youth that I thought was locked in the recesses up here.' He tapped his head.

Skeeter stood and her facial expression clearly showed interest. 'Confession time?' She smiled for the first time that morning.

He chuckled again. 'The guilty pleasure was nothing more than comics, to be exact. I was an avid reader, superheroes, especially Batman and The Joker.' He paused as if to question why he was saying this at such a critical time. 'The Joker. Did you know he was originally known as Red Hood? Sorry, I digress, but not a lot of people know that. Forgive me.' He shook his head. 'Anyway, when I saw the bikers in the news it brought it to mind then, too.' There was another pause, and Skeeter chose deliberately not to fill it. 'So, seeing this was one of those déjà vu moments. I did find something though. Our man here was carrying a debit card in the arm pocket of his jogging jacket. I put it back. Registered to a Mr C Jenkins. Interestingly, there was an audio bud close to the body, too.' Mott pointed to the piece of white plastic positioned near the obelisk base. 'I presumed it could be his but nothing's certain. Might have been lost as his head struck.'

Skeeter leaned forward and inspected the object. 'The other is probably in there somewhere,' she pointed to the now re-covered head. 'Any sign of a phone?'

'Not that I'm aware. My colleague here turned and patted down the body to check for other injuries and they'd have felt a phone, surely. There was no sign.' He shook his head, as did his colleague. 'As I said before, you'll be expecting a doctor as there's nothing more I can do here.' He flashed a smile and started to collect his equipment and bag. 'You have my details. Our body cams have recorded the whole procedure. I'll organise my report as soon as.'

'Yes, thanks for your help. Owing to the circumstances, the coroner will be informed.' As she spoke CSI arrived.

Turning away, she called April.

'All evidence suggests suspicious circumstances, another murder.' She knew the statement sounded foolish considering the evidence she had seen. She realised the danger of presump-tion. 'The victim is possibly a Mr C Jenkins. Paramedic found a debit card. I have the details to help us track him. There's no phone. However, an Apple-style ear bud, an AirPod, was found close to the body, but if it was his, and there was no sign of a phone …'

'Doctor will be with you shortly. I'll notify the coroner.' April was eager to end the call.

'Something else. The paramedic mentioned The Joker and Red Hood. It made the hair on my neck stand. Hasn't Michael been banging on about that? The medic had been an avid comic reader in his youth.'

'Do you have a name?'

'Chris Mott. First responder.' Skeeter sounded quizzical.

'Thanks. Organise a briefing for four this afternoon, please.'

* * *

DC Colin Drake sat opposite John Rathbone, whose feet bounced uncontrollably beneath the chair as he played with his hands. If Colin had a pound for every time he had witnessed this nervous behaviour, he would be a rich man. Kasum sat slightly away from the table, as if impartial. She maintained a steady smile. Colin went through Rathbone's basic details confirming name and address, only receiving confirmation when pushed. He quickly realised the interview would not be dissimilar to plaiting soot.

'We don't know you, Mr Rathbone. You have no history with us. Well done! So, why now? Remember, you've been cautioned, and this interview is being recorded as evidence on this case and for your own safety.' Colin Drake never let his facial expression change as he looked directly at John, who had found difficulty keeping eye contact from the outset. 'Where were you yesterday morning, Mr Rathbone, from let's say, nine until eleven?' He leaned back and folded his arms.

Rathbone looked down at his hands and allowed his thumbs to roll over each other. 'I was home.'

Drake turned an iPad round and pressed play. The CCTV of the raid was clear to see. At a key point, he paused it. His finger fell on one of the attackers. 'That, Mr Rathbone, is you.'

Rathbone leaned back and folded his arms. He closed his eyes as he shook his head.

'No? That person, we are accurately informed, is five foot

ten. Weighs about seventy-six kilos. Same build as you. You have a tattoo on your left hand. The letters 0AA.'

The lad frowned and quickly hid his hand beneath the other.

'That's how we know that person with the object in his hand is you. When we used our forensic digital AI capabilities, we could see it. The letters 0AA on that finger of your right hand.' Drake also leaned forward and spread his fingers whilst pointing to the location on his own finger.

'I was wearing—'

'Gloves? You were, yes, you were wearing gloves. Was that what you were about to say? Have you ever been through security at an airport? I know you have. From your passport record we've deduced that you went to Spain last September. You travelled from John Lennon Airport with your mum and your auntie. We know a lot, you see. Do you remember standing with your feet on the markers and being asked to spread your arms? Well, that process allows the Border Force to see you, almost naked, and therefore they can see what's on your body.' Drake paused and glanced at Kasum knowing she would play along. 'Now, imagine, Mr Rathbone, if our street cameras could do the same. It wouldn't matter if you wore gloves or not. This man in the video is you. The three letter tattoo confirms it.'

Rathbone looked at his hands and then at Kasum who smiled and cocked her head to the side.

'Let's make this easy for you as you have no criminal history. The others in custody have. Pleading guilty and offering a full confession will likely bring bail and a short, suspended sentence. That would mean no prison time if you keep your nose clean. Nobody would know you'd said anything. However, to help with their plea, the others might want to link you to the death of a woman who was possibly connected to one of the robberies in which you all were involved. Now that, Mr Rathbone, would be a different ball game. It could make you an accessory to murder.' He let out a low, long whistle. 'Murder. Now we're getting really serious.' He stood. 'I have to leave the room briefly, but you will be with the custody officer and DC Kapoor here. I'll be about ten minutes. Let's hope none of the others says too much before I get back.'

Drake left the room.

* * *

The morning traffic was busy as Tony pulled up on Dale Street and parked partly on the pavement. The pub was on his right. The area, once busy with traditional pubs, had changed out of all proportion. The wine bars and restaurants had taken over. Checking the road, he crossed. He was just a few minutes late. As requested, he went to the door that was positioned down a narrow, cobbled alleyway. It was open. He was immediately hit by that traditional pub aroma, but he also could clearly smell disinfectant.

A man mopping the wooden floor looked up as he entered. 'You from the police?'

Tony held his ID before looking at the freshly mopped floor.

'You're okay, it's done and will be done again tomorrow whether it needs it or not. The woman you mentioned sat in that corner.' He pointed before resting the mop against the bar. 'We've found and copied the CCTV footage requested for that date. Focusing on the times you gave, we apparently had one female who came in alone.' Moving behind the bar he collected a laptop. 'Here we go.'

Tony moved closer.

'Came in and ordered what looks like a gin and tonic and then moved to that seat there. It was lunchtime and quite busy. Looking at her coat, I imagine it was raining. The bloke with the brolly you can see at the bar, came in a few minutes after her. There, he's the one wearing a baseball cap and glasses.'

Tony watched the video without saying anything further. He recognised Caitlin. Watching her remove her phone, it appeared she had made a call. From the interview with Steph, she had mentioned Caitlin had called her from the pub.

'The chap at the bar goes over to her. There see.'

On occasion, the number of people standing and milling around the small room concealed Caitlin. From what Tony could see from her body language, the man appeared to be a stranger to her. As if deliberate, the man's face was always positioned away from the camera. 'Can you rewind so we can get a clearer shot of his face?'

Even when rewound at a slower pace, it was clear to Tony the man had deliberately avoided the camera, keeping his head down or away from the CCTV.

'Do you just have the one camera?' Tony pointed to the darkened dome positioned in the ceiling to the left of the bar.

'No, we have one that monitors the till and there's one covering the rear door in the alleyway. There was one a while back over by the far corner, but it stopped working. I was always meaning to get it fixed but ...'

Tony thanked the landlord, slipped the memory stick of the video images into his pocket and left. Maybe digital forensics could get a clearer image or profile to run on the facial recognition software. It always made him wonder why NASA could achieve clear footage from deep in space and yet some CCTV could only achieve footage as if taken in fog even though the camera and the subject were mere metres apart. It would, he felt, be forever one of the mysteries of science.

* * *

'I don't know who he was and that's the truth.' John Rathbone let his eyes linger on Kasum for longer than a few moments and for the first time since the interview had commenced. 'Honest, none of us knew who he was or why he was doing it. Not even …'

'Not even the one who tells you what to do, John?' Kasum prompted.

He nodded. 'Nobody did. He used to phone and then leave cash and instructions, notes in places to be collected. I don't know where. I also don't know nothing about the woman. We just robbed stuff.'

'You used force. You saw the blade.' Kasum put her elbows on the table before resting her chin on her hands. It brought her closer to Rathbone but that was deliberate. 'Were you the one with the blade, John.'

His shake of the head was tentative. 'We got a bollocking for that. No weapons, no blades we were told. We were robbing, shoplifting, that's all. Honest, I never harmed no one.'

'You know one shop assistant grabbed the person with the weapon. We have that person's DNA and because you've been charged, we have your DNA, too. Let's hope they don't match, John.'

'I didn't do that. Cross my heart.'

'Tell me about the hoods, John.'

There was a pause of uncertainty. 'It was his idea.'

'Whose?'

'The Controller, the one who paid and got nowt from the robberies. He left a roll of the red cloth. It was like the stuff used for sacking. He also left other coloured cotton material and instructions of how to make them and a drawing of what they should look like. We didn't have them at first. It was only when he interfered. He told us they had to be sewn onto jumpers to stop them being pulled off.'

Kasum pushed two photographs from the file across the

table. The first showed the hoods with one face, the second with two. John looked at each and a kind of smile crossed his lips.

'Why add a second face?' She touched the relevant photograph.

'I love sewing.' He blushed. 'My nan taught me when I wanted to put patches on a denim jacket. I really enjoyed it. She said I'd make a good tailor.' His grin gave away his immaturity and pride. 'It was the first time I could do anything proper, like, the first time anyone said something I'd done was good. I was always crap at school. Do you know, people laughed at me. They said I was thick. Some teachers, too. Hated it. Sewing was different but I thought it was for girls. I was frightened to tell them until … Once they saw my hood, they were dead impressed … Made me feel ten feet tall, and for once I actually felt important.'

She smiled, it was sincere. 'So why two faces?'

'That was my idea. Funny really. A while back I was in Asda and there was a chap in front of me. I thought he was staring at me all the time. Whenever I looked up, he was looking straight back at me.' He chuckled for the first time since entering the interview room. 'I realised that he was bald, and he'd had a full, human-sized face tattooed on the back of his head. It freaked me out when I realised. When I'd made my hood and after the first …' He paused realising he was saying too much. 'Anyway, I decided I'd use the idea, I'd add another face to the back. The others liked it, so I did theirs, too.'

'You sewed all the hoods?' As she spoke, she saw him nod whilst she retrieved another photograph from the file. 'Did you make this one, John?'

John looked at the image. It was of the mask retrieved from the Gormley figure. She could immediately understand the negative look on his face.

'Is this a joke?' He tossed the photograph onto the desk and folded his arms as if setting a barrier between them. He looked insulted.

'It's not one of yours is it, John?'

He shook his head.

'Why isn't it one of yours?'

'Because it's shite. Look at it!' Releasing his arms, he tapped the photograph with a finger. 'Because I can fucking sew. Whoever did that has obviously used glue and a few shit stitches. They've done a crap job. I wouldn't wipe my arse with it.'

It was Kasum's turn to sit back. She could detect echoes from his schooling in his anger. Before her was a boy who had been broken and robbed of his confidence. She also realised why he become part of a gang – to feel wanted.

* * *

Alan Green read the instructions for about the fourth time. It hardly made any sense. He knew the locations, but the task seemed ludicrous. The date and time seemed to have no relevance, it was just over a week away – the opening evening of The River of Light Festival. He had never heard of it and, had he, he would still have not been interested. Not only did the person making the request seem ridiculous, the latest instructions were even more obscure. The one consolation was he could just walk away, keep what money he had been given and go. Besides, the police might just call anytime and the whole idea would be buried. Folding up the instructions, he stood. He rang home. According to his mother, it was safe to return.

CHAPTER 23

It was just after 4pm and the briefing room was full. The buzz of conversation reflected the number of people within the room and the curiosity the case was beginning to generate. The evidence on the whiteboards had increased significantly. It was ordered, chronological and structured. A number of officers took notes from the latest additions. April stood and tapped the table. The chatter immediately subsided.

'Thanks. As you're aware, we now have a second victim, but, more than likely, they're actually the third victim as we're still investigating the disappearance of Ghulam. Early today the body of a Mr Carl Jenkins, a thirty-three year old male, was discovered in Sefton Park. He'd suffered the same injuries as manifested on Caitlin Byrne. However, you can see from this image...' Behind, on the screen, a photograph of the hooded corpse was displayed. 'On this occasion, the red hood was added after a polythene bag had been placed over the victim's head. Asphyxiation has been confirmed as the cause of death. Time of death is currently set at between five and six this morning. Jenkins also suffered a severe injury to the back of the skull. It's believed this resulted from his striking his head when falling, after being struck on the left side of his chin, probably. According to preliminary tests, it was the only blow. The same pattern as before.'

'Was the body dumped? The park is busy even at that godforsaken hour,' Phil quizzed.

April checked her notes. 'Considering he'd been out running, he was probably attacked where he fell. Interestingly, he was wearing AirPods. One remained intact, whilst the other was found close to the body. There was no phone found on the body and a thorough search of the area has also failed to locate it. We're assuming it was stolen, but then why kill someone so elaborately if theft is the motive? His phone records show the last call he made was yesterday evening, which was to a friend, and it's been confirmed. Next of kin have also been informed.'

'A bike snatch?' someone asked without real conviction. A number of heads turned. 'It happens all the time,' he appealed in defence of his initial question. 'Running with a phone can make you an easy target.'

'Keeping an open mind is key, and so nothing can be ruled out at this early stage. Kasum, can you continue?' April sat as Kasum moved to the front.

'Several members of the bike gang, the Red Hoods, have been interviewed, but there's one in particular, his name is John Rathbone. No previous, and, if I'm honest, he's a very worried chap. He quickly admitted to making all of the hoods for the group.'

There was immediate chatter, but it settled as she raised a hand. 'However, he denied making the one found on the Gormley figure.' She documented his reasons. 'A further forensic inspection of that item supports his assertion. He did refuse to say where his is kept, if it still exists.'

'Did he say where the material came from?' Tony asked as he removed a piece of fingernail with his teeth.

'The mystery man. The Controller. Left it in a safe place for collection, as he did with the payments and instructions. Forensics have identified the material, and we're investigating suppliers. It's the colour that's the issue. There's a slight variation on the first one found and whether that's due to the elements or the dying process we're unsure. Forensics are looking into that, too. It could well prove to be home-dyed material.'

'So, this controller has manipulated these kamikaze robbers to dance to his tune? Red hoods and maybe the moniker. A proper puppet master of sorts,' Tony added. 'The more we discover, the more I think there's a strong link to what Michael suggested with the comic.'

'His thalamus theory,' April added before continuing. 'Anything from the others in custody?'

'As yet, no. We still have time. We await the DNA match from the blade attacker with those now in custody. Colin is questioning each, searching for their Achilles' heels.'

'Thanks, Kasum.' April looked across at DC Lucy Teraoka who stood in anticipation.

'We know this style of kamikaze robbery has been on the increase for some time, not necessarily with bikes, but they are on the increase, as are the small gangs who enter shops and commit theft as if it's a game. We know why, too. Many are stealing to order, knowing there's a shortage of officers on the ground, and, therefore, little chance of being apprehended. Staff, too, have been instructed not to get involved, on health and safety grounds, and response times are slow, I'm sad to say. To begin with, Michael Peet suggested I focus on the bike attacks, single and multiple within our area over the last twelve to eighteen months. Looking back, one seemed to stand out as it resulted in the death of a young woman, a Kate Nolan.' She studied her notes. 'It occurred about eleven months ago, and from the evidence we have, it was really a robbery that went badly wrong. A bag snatch, and we've had many of those as well as the snatching of phones, but this one resulted in Nolan being thrown beneath the wheels of a moving heavy goods vehicle. The two responsible were on an electric motorbike. They were never caught, and obviously the case is still open.' She paused. 'What's more interesting is, according to Michael, there were a number of witnesses as it was a busy lunchtime attack. It appeared that not only did people try to help, but, as always, elements of the incident were videoed. He believes, and there's evidence to suggest this, that some of those videos were posted on various social media platforms. They were swiftly removed owing to the graphic nature of the content, some by those posting but others by the admin of the sites. They can, once posted, be shared like wildfire. He's investigating if we can get that footage recovered or at least the names of those responsible. I also believe, in the light of our present cases, we should interview the witnesses of the incident again.'

'I take it none of those who posted was injured themselves?' April quizzed, knowing her question was a long shot.

'Not as far as we're aware, but I still feel it's an avenue we must not close down.' Lucy looked around the room as if searching for support.

'Okay, Lucy. Please chase that and work with Skeeter wherever possible. Keep us informed.' April thanked everyone but was interrupted as Skeeter stood.

'I must, at this stage, return to what Tony's just said. During this morning's investigation, Michael's theory raised its head again as the First Responder offered his thoughts after seeing the victim. He mirrored Michael Peet's theory regarding the fictitious character, Red Hood. The more we discover, the more the finer elements of the story seem to get stronger and more relevant. None of the members of the gang would have any idea about Red Hood even if they know about Batman. If I'm honest, I would never have linked them, as I'm sure many people in here didn't until Michael brought it up. Somehow, I believe it to be a key element that we could easily dismiss, but I strongly believe we should investigate further.'

April closed the meeting. 'I'll speak to Michael. Let's see if there are any links with the broader and newer elements of the case, in particular, Carl Jenkins' death and maybe now, Kate Nolan's. Thanks everyone.' There was initial silence as she left the room, and the chatter soon erupted as the room cleared.

* * *

The interviews were going slowly. Colin Drake was nothing if not meticulous in his questioning, but the reluctance of the people he was dealing with to co-operate made it torturous. It was a process he often likened to chess. Even though he had no evidence to link any of those in custody with the deaths of either of the recent victims, he knew, and so did their duty solicitors, there was still a possible link. Murder was a leverage tool he could use when all else failed. He watched the video of Skeeter's interview with Crabtree before entering the interview room.

Drake sat opposite and smiled at the duty solicitor who immediately raised an eyebrow.

'Mr Crabtree has assured me, DC Drake, he is sorry for his previous outbursts towards the female detective and is willing to co-operate fully.'

Crabtree leaned back in his chair. The undamaged eye stared back with a degree of defiance, whereas his other was now half-closed owing to the swelling. Drake slid a photograph of Caitlin Byrne across the table.

'Do you recognise this woman?'

He leaned forward, briefly scanned the image and shook his head.

'Please answer.'

'No.'

'She witnessed one of your robberies. She was standing less than ten feet from you. You even looked directly at her at one point.'

'I've told you ... No. Loads of people were there, you know that.' He looked at his solicitor. 'I'm telling the truth. Who is she?'

'She was murdered after watching you.' Drake let the answer hang. The mood in the room changed abruptly, as quickly as did Crabtree's expression.

'I knew about it. I knew it had happened. They knew, too. We only heard on the news. Frightened us all shitless.' He placed his hands on the table, his good eye swiftly travelling to both men. 'There's someone behind the group,' he paused as if searching his conscience, considering how much he should reveal.

'As your legal representative, I would advise you to tell the officer everything you know. Withholding information, at this stage, can only create more problems for you in the future. If you do not tell the truth now, Mr Crabtree, you'll have to have an extremely good memory in the future.' The duty solicitor spoke slowly ensuring every word was fully understood.

Crabtree's whole demeanour changed. 'Look, I just do as I'm told ... But there's a bloke ... he's known to us as The Controller, and, before you ask, I don't know who he is, where he is or even what he looks like. He came on the scene a while back, and I was worried then, but he paid good money and, therefore, he sets the jobs and gives the instructions, but he takes nothing. He insisted we do the red hoods.'

'Those hoods. You don't make the hoods. Rathbone does. He sews them all. Instructions from your controller.' As Colin spoke, he watched as Crabtree's look of uncertainty flushed. His body language instantly softened. 'You see, we know more than you think. Those who co-operate are looked on with a degree of leniency. It's all about give and take.'

Crabtree frowned, clearly now even more insecure.

'To be honest, we're chasing a killer, but you're not helping. According to you, this is what we know. No one has seen him. He rings, leaves instructions or the material in a set place. When the job is done, the same happens, only this time money is left along with further instructions. Is that correct so far?'

'Who told you?'

'You're the only one who's failed to co-operate with this very serious case, and that's a shame. It suggests guilt, and it puts you out on a limb, so to speak. We ...' he pointed to the solicitor and then at himself, 'only want what's best for you. We want the killer, and I believe at this stage it's neither you nor anyone else in the gang but until we have evidence, you're all in serious trouble, lad, but then you know that, as something in here tells me,' he pointed to his stomach. 'It makes me believe there's something else you could tell me to help us get to the bottom of the lady's death. I believe you are not the killer.' He leaned forward as if to consolidate his pronouncement.

Crabtree did not know whether to nod or shake his head. 'Thank you, I didn't do it.' He burst into tears.

'Now, Mr Crabtree, are you the one who receives the messages? If not, who is?'

CHAPTER 24

The whole of the Mersey estuary spread out before him for one hundred and eighty degrees; its pewter-coloured surface, ripped and torn by the occasional lines of silver, clearly fashioned by the wind and the tidal currents. The river here was trapped at its widest point before curving and snaking inland. The cutting of the Manchester Ship Canal had severed a tranche of land, left to nature, known as Stanlow Island, green and isolated running along the river's edge. Once it had been inhabited by monks, the ruins of the monastery were still visible, and then the canal police occupied the area for some time; they, too, had left their mark. The derelict police station could be seen from this vantage point. The island was now deserted other than by the mariners whose boats arrive to be filled from the Essar Petroleum works positioned on the opposite bank, or by the bird counters who arrive for a few days every year.

He was immediately distracted as a flock of birds swooped in a broad arc across the canal, the full flight descending to land collectively along the brown mudflat left by the receding tide. That one action seemed to bring more birds, all eager to search the tide's bounty. Considering the location so close to the heavily industrialised area, the island remained a haven of green and natural beauty. Any trace of man was slowly being swallowed into the vegetation. Allowing his eyes to focus more closely on the building brought a very different perspective. The collection of pipe-works, gantries and industrial detritus left little place for the natural world, other than for weeds and the occasional stunted tree.

The view from the office was in constant flux, either from the changing light or the contrasting weather. Each day, even though the refinery surrounded the site, the vista seemed to enhance rather than detract. His hand moved to the knot of his tie, and he adjusted it whilst catching a vague reflection from the window. Even though he still found the river and the sea beautiful, it was impossible to look at water for long, no matter where or in what form, without an emotional light boring into the recess of his memory. It always turned back the clock and allowed his mind's eye to focus on a specific, dark day. With professional help, effort, and with the gradual passage of time, he could sometimes turn off that light and leave his mind in the dark and at peace. Occasionally, when he felt weak and vulnerable, he was forced to leave the light on. It was part of the healing process he had been assured he would experience. Now was one of those moments. He moved to his desk and let his mind wander.

For a spring day, a bank holiday, if he recalled correctly, it had been chill, and even though the sun had flooded the promenade with long shadows, he remembered how the cutting wind had found gaps in his clothing as it had swirled in strong gusts. He had dressed in the appropriate number of layers, but still he'd felt its bite. With his elbows on the desk, he rested his chin on his hands. He closed his eyes and the past, his past returned. The second of the two worst days he had ever experienced came flooding back. It was not the only tragedy that triggered his hatred, but the first chronologically, and in some ways, the most prophetic.

The bright blue of the sky and the low, milky spring sun had been deceptive. The sun had offered little heat. The tide was high and the wind, although not seemingly strong, brought the water crashing over the brown, concrete lip of the promenade, a huge burst that cascaded along its length. At this point, the sloping concrete wall held multicoloured wooden planks, forming seats that faced away from the sea. Owing to the unforeseeable overspray, they were empty. The occasional shelter could be seen much further along and seemed a more appropriate spot to rest and take in the view. Considering the cold, the promenade was busy. Joggers, cyclists and dog walkers prevailed, as well as a few kids daring each other to beat the cascading waves, waves that were unpredictable and varied in strength and force. The squeals of daring excitement from three kids were loud and shrill. They were clearly oblivious to the chill and the wet, the fun was in the challenge. It was at that moment, a moment when he had stopped to admire Fort Perch Rock Fort and the lighthouse some distance away, now surrounded by the beating surf, that it all started – when his day changed. It was the intensity of the screams that seemed so altered, they were more excited and urgent, making him turn sharply. Three children were dashing through the break in the wall, disappearing down the steps that would normally lead to the beach; but today, at high tide, the lower reaches were well below the water line. There they waited, watching the huge incoming waves, before dashing back up the steps to break out onto the prom, a place of relative safety. The waves eagerly followed, crashing against the side of the steps, chasing them back up before exploding over the wall in a huge, opaque cascade. Their laughter was shrill, mimicking the gulls' calls, a constant chorus alongside the crescendo of crashing water on concrete. As their daring grew, each descent took them lower and closer to the water's edge.

From the corner of his eye, he watched as only two of the children escaped onto the promenade from the top of the steps. Once there, their laughter seemed more subdued and uncertain. He waited for the third child, the only girl in the group, to make an appearance. All he saw was another huge plume of sea spray crashing heavily onto the ground around them, as myriad droplets innocently broke into multiple mini rainbows as the low sun penetrated the spray. He, and four other people who were nearby, immediately realised there was a problem. Dashing over to the sea wall, the sea was wild, and his worst fear unfolded before his eyes. The child was now well away from the bottom of the steps and held within the deep and violent water. Her arms flailing and increasingly, her head kept disappearing below the sea's surface like another piece of flotsam. Screams beat at his ears as he grabbed the life ring attached to the right side of the steps, throwing it towards the drowning child. Its arching trajectory battled against the wind and the force was inadequate. It landed too short. To pull it back and try again, he sensed, would take too long.

Slipping off his overcoat and shoes, he shouted for someone to call 999 as he carefully navigated the now slippery, concrete steps, trying to anticipate when the next wave would strike. For some bizarre reason, the scene from *Papillon* came to mind, even in the middle of his moment of panic. The girl's scream brought him back to reality. With luck, he hoped the child would be carried closer to him, but he soon realised that would not be the case. She was being swept further away. Not knowing the depth of water, he slipped into the foaming sea whilst gripping the steps. The cold immediately stole his breath, and the salt water stung his eyes. Scanning the ever-moving surface, he saw the girl's arm appear from the foaming water as he swam towards her, his head above the surface, his flailing arms eagerly striking out with all his might in her direction. The spray from the onshore wind whipped his face, blurring his vision. That, in concert with the strong tide, made the swim harder than he could ever imagine. After seconds that seemed like minutes, he grabbed the child, swiftly turning her so that her head rested high on his chest and above the waterline. Only one of the many who were spectating had run down the steps, pulled in the lifebelt and tossed it out again, whilst keeping hold of the attached rope. The red-and-white ring landed just in front of him. Desperately, he grabbed. Success gave him a minute's respite as he bobbed in the corrugated surf. He no longer felt the cold. Looking up at the promenade wall, a larger crowd had gathered, and, to his dismay and anger, he noticed a number were videoing the unfolding drama and his desperate struggle to keep her head out of the water, to keep her alive. He froze, as if his world had stopped again. He could neither move one way nor the other. It was as if he were about to sink. Had it not been for one person who had shown initiative, retrieved the belt and called out whilst the others watched, he might have given up. He watched as occasionally the ghoulish spectators disappeared from sight as another wave crashed over the wall before them.

The shout, the desperation of the good Samaritan, brought a return of his survival mode. He held onto the ring. In seconds, he was pulled in towards the steps. Two more people disregarded their own safety and braved the heavy spray, the slippery steps and the crashing waves, to come to his assistance. The water he had involuntarily swallowed seemed to fill his lungs, giving few opportunities to grab his breath. The child seemed motionless, trapped between his arm and chest.

The gradual sound of sirens overpowered the pounding of the crashing water as he passed the child to one of the people on the steps. He briefly trod water, always fearful the next incoming wave would force his body uncontrollably against the concrete and wash him back out before he could manage to find both foot and hand holds. To his relief, more rescuing arms pulled him clear of the water and towards the higher steps, away from the sea but not the exploding waves. Although many people clapped as he appeared and collapsed on the promenade, two people continued to film.

Wrapped in a foil blanket, his body still shivered even though he did not feel cold. His whole being felt numb. He watched as one man continued to video the efforts of the emergency services as they worked on the child. He shouted his protest.

The press coverage had been intense and short-lived. The word 'hero' had been used on more than one occasion, but he had not managed to save the girl. It was then that the guilt had crept in. The questions accosted him over and over again. If he had gone in sooner, would she still be alive? Had he managed to throw the lifebelt more accurately, would she have lived? If he had swum faster? If others had been of more help? Each nagging doubt multiplied in his mind. The thoughts were an intrusion when time hung heavily and the level in the bottle fell. It was only after the medical intervention, the counsellor that offered a clearer perspective, could his demons be laid to rest so life could continue. However, he knew there would always be a scar, and, with that, a growing resentment. For some time afterwards, he had also held a fear of drowning that was buried deeply in his past, and, with it, the anger and inner resentment.

He rubbed his eyes to remove the mental images, images that had plagued him ever since. They had diagnosed PTSD. He allowed his focus to fall on the personal items that filled his desk surface. He touched the photograph, a duplicate of the one he had at home, and the one, that at times like these, meant so much.

He never thought he would admit this to himself, but it was

good to be back in this place, at this desk; it was the only work he had known since finishing his doctorate at university. Computer science had always been his passion. In this place was a security, an invisible commonality. People knew him, and he knew them. This sense of familiarity brought a half smile.

He shivered, again, at the memory as he checked his phone. From an earlier news report, he knew the body had been found. However, few details had been revealed. His mind flashed back to the prostrate figure and the red hood. The usual nausea returned. He had felt so anxious being in such a public space as so much had been left to chance. The first victim had been relatively easy to entice. His name flashed through his mind followed by the face of Ghulam Mohammed. It was the young man's disappointment and confusion that had been so evident; he would never forget. Ghulam had been expecting a young woman, a woman who had befriended him after seeing his post of the shop robbery on social media. It was to be a date full of promises, all so convenient, so enticing. To watch the man turn, expecting to find a moment of promised pleasure only for it to morph into the man's worst nightmare, had proved so exhilarating.

Once Ghulam was reported missing, there had never been much enthusiasm on the police's part to investigate, after all, asylum seekers vanish all of the time, especially those who know they have little chance of a successful claim for asylum. If the police were to search for each one who went walkabout, then there would be no time for anything else. If he were honest, he had hoped he would be discovered, even though back then there was no red hood.

Turning the key, he opened his desk drawer. The three phones belonging to the victims were positioned in order. All now slept. He removed the dog-eared comic that he had placed within a manilla file; it was for his eyes only. He remembered the day he had seen it for the first time in the second-hand book shop in Chester. It had been the cover, the simple drawing of a red-hooded figure that had sparked his interest, and, much later, the idea. That, and the link within the story to the chemical works, had been the reason he had spent more money than he could justify to purchase it. The comic book's character, who was wearing the red hood, had failed whilst trying to escape, failed to hang onto Batman's hand, a helping hand from his adversary. He had fallen into a vat of chemical waste, and although there were no such vats here, in his place of work, the seed had been sown, and the idea took up residence in his own head. Trapped within the comic's pages were two newspaper cuttings. He read the headline of the first: Local Man Hailed as a Super Hero. The article detailed his valiant effort to save the child. He replaced it, taking out the second one that was older. His office door opened.

'Working late?' Mark Hayes, a colleague, leaned into his office.

Instinctively, he sheltered the comic with his arms as Mark approached. 'I've nearly done.'

Mark giggled as he spoke. 'Are you hiding a mucky mag, my friend?' He pointed to the desk.

'I wish,' he laughed. 'Old comic.' He turned to show the cover.

Mark leaned forward to get a better look. 'Who the hell's that?'

'To do with Batman. I picked it up in a second-hand book shop in Chester a short while ago and never took it home. Read them when I was a kid. My dad kept loads. Then I was fascinated by Dan Dare. I guess that's where the spark originated, why I got into computers. Stephen liked them, too.'

'Stephen?'

He did not respond as he opened the desk drawer and slipped in the magazine. It created an awkward silence.

'I'm going for a beer. Can I tempt you?' Mark looked out of the window as he spoke. 'I never tire of this view.'

'Beer? No, but I'll join you and have a coffee. My medication and alcohol should not be mixed. They say it could make me aggressive,' he winked. 'Mucky mag, indeed. Do they still sell them in corner newsagents?'

'Do they still have corner newsagents?' Mark riposted.

He turned the key in the lock, checked the drawer was secure, stood, and they left the office together.

'Vape shops now, I guess. Everything's digital.'

Their laughter faded as they walked down the corridor.

CHAPTER 25

The day had seemed endless as Skeeter leaned on the side of the porch door to her cottage. A mug of green tea steamed as she stared at the irregular stone pathway that led to the gate. The old tree, although large, was twisted and bent having the appearance of a giant Bonsai. The sky remained grey, but the temperature contradicted the ambience it shed. She felt an excited flutter in her stomach. Steve would be back from his time in Leeds. He would be full of enthusiasm for the new drone he had been evaluating, and she knew the evening's conversation would be predominantly technical.

'Daydreaming, lass?' The voice interrupted her thoughts.

'Bloody hell, Tom. I bet you can walk on rice paper without leaving a mark!'

Tom was her elderly neighbour. Their paths were separated by an immaculately trimmed privet hedge. Tom's path was lower so he could not be seen but was often heard. If Tom were out, he was either gardening or smoking, usually the latter.

'Saw you a while back, Skeeter, as I was feeding the birds. You seemed miles away. That fella of yours not back yet?' He lit a cigarette, and the smoke drifted up and over the hedge. Skeeter smelt the rich tobacco.

'He is, later today, Tom. That's not your usual smoke.'

'Ground compost and oak leaves this one, lass,' he chuckled. 'Good for the joints I'm informed.'

Skeeter chuckled, too. 'I could get used to that aroma.' She watched as the smoke drifted further down the path in dying, grey wisps.

'The missus couldn't, she hates the smell of any tobacco, that's why I'm banished here to the wilderness, no matter the weather. Says it'll stain the ceiling and walls yellow if I smoke indoors, and yet she still has an open fire. Why can I never fathom women's logic?' He did not wait for an answer. 'Still, I get to chat to you so that makes up for it. Caught those daft robbing bastards on motorbikes yet? Saw it on the telly. What's with the red hoods?'

'We have some in custody, but not all of them. The red hoods are a bit of a mystery.'

'Give 'em a clip round the bloody lughole from me, that's what they're short of. Saw some the other day on the lane here. Riding on the back wheel, no helmets. Strange thing was that the bikes were silent. They'll kill someone soon. You mark my words.'

The noise of the gate latch made Skeeter look towards the road; it was Steve. He was carrying a bunch of flowers and a bottle. A broad grin was splashed across his face.

'I think he's missed you, lass. He's obviously a keeper. I should really take notes but …' The large plume of smoke appeared as he took his last drag before flicking the cigarette butt into the sand bucket by the door. 'I think my tea's ready.' He threw up a hand as if in salute and disappeared inside.

Skeeter trotted up the path and hugged Steve. Neither spoke for a few minutes.

'Good to be back,' he whispered as he kissed her. 'Missed you.' He held out the flowers. 'They're not from the petrol station either before you make some smart-ass comment.'

Skeeter shook her head.

'Wine, too, your favourite.'

She took the flowers and his hand. 'Need a drink? Meal's in the slow cooker.'

'Thought you'd never ask.'

* * *

The interview room seemed particularly dark. The lack of any creature comforts allowed the acoustics to mimic those of a bathroom. Colin Drake sat opposite Mick Webster and the duty solicitor. He deliberately spread the documents onto the table before collecting them. Drake looked at Webster and then at the solicitor, who had been briefed.

'Mr Webster,' he smiled as he spoke. 'Do you own one of these?'

He removed a photograph of a kitchen sharpening steel from the file. Turning it, he pushed it in front of Webster, who continued to look at his hands and remain unresponsive.

'Mr Webster?'

'Mr Webster was my old man, and he was an evil bastard. Micky. I've told you, I answer to Micky.'

Drake looked at the solicitor and then back at Webster. He collected the photograph and slipped it back into the file. 'I take it that's a yes, Mr Webster.' He then removed another photograph showing a still image taken from CCTV of the attack on the member of staff. He pushed that across the table.

'We believe that's you, Micky.' He tapped the photograph with his finger.

Webster pulled a face as he picked up the photograph before turning it round, pointing to the hood and then his own face. 'I don't think I look like that. What do you think?' He smirked before tossing the photograph back across the table.

'We know that person is you. We were fortunate to get a DNA sample from that attack. It was under the fingernails of the poor man whom you stabbed. As you know, Micky,' he broke the word down into syllables, highlighting his demand. 'We took the DNA of all those we have in custody, your mates. We have a match. Now that tells us that the man in the mask is the same person as one of the people we have in custody. Believe the science, Micky, it's never wrong.'

Webster shuffled and looked at his solicitor, the disgruntled frown clearly showing on his face.

'You're the winner of that challenge, Micky. You were the one who used a weapon causing grievous bodily harm. You're a dangerous man, and you are now under further arrest as the offence with which we expect to charge you has just escalated. It's now very serious.' He turned towards the custody officer who moved forward.

'Fuck yourself, copper. What about the others?'

Drake held up his hand and the custody officer paused.

'They didn't try to kill anyone, as far as we know. However, we have clear evidence to show that you did. If you could attempt to kill the man at the store, then logic says you could kill the woman who videoed you doing just that.'

'Not me, not a woman. I'd never do that.' He turned to his solicitor seeking reassurance. 'What about the others?' Micky's voice had lost its previous confidence.

'As I said, they robbed but didn't attack anyone. They'll be post-charge bailed.' Drake collected his file. 'Probably when they go to court, they'll receive a suspended sentence dependent on their police records. However, you, Micky, will face a prison sentence. Robbery with violence and causing grievous bodily harm are very serious offences. You're just lucky you didn't kill the man.'

'I didn't do the hoods, didn't pick the places …' He paused.

'No, Rathbone made the hoods. Crabtree told us what he could about The Controller. We also know that no weapons should have been carried. You ignored that instruction didn't you, Micky? You knew better as you're the hard man in the group. But then, according to what we've heard from your friends, you do tend to plough your own furrow.'

Micky frowned as he folded his arms.

To Drake, he looked like a petulant child.

'You could still help yourself and tell us the names of all the gang. We know many of them and I'm sure we'll soon know them all.'

Micky pushed his lip out a little further.

Drake picked up the file. 'I'm late for home. You'll be staying here. Should you wish to chat with your solicitor, I'm sure he'll be all ears, and for what it's worth, whatever professional, legal advice he offers you, I'd listen if I were you, but more importantly, I'd heed.'

On returning to his desk, Drake found an urgent note.

The DNA sample will be inadmissible in this case owing to cross contamination at the scene.

'Fuck!'

* * *

Skeeter finished loading the dishwasher as Steve poured more drinks.

'That was wonderful, thank you.' He moved through to the lounge, the wood burner cast an orange glow along the low wooden beams. 'So, this case you're working on, what's with the red hoods?'

'An instruction from the guy who appears to be controlling the gang. He pays them but takes nothing from the robberies. We believe he's present at the robbery sites owing to his ridiculous attempt to hide his identity as a member of the public. There's a chance he was also in the same pub as the woman, the lunchtime she died, but at present that's speculative.'

'Might be ludicrous but if you don't know who he is, his ridiculous attempt at concealment seems to be working.'

Skeeter shrugged her shoulders. 'The weird thing is the death —' Her phone rang. It was April.

'Sorry it's late but thought you'd like to know, the guy you found this morning had posted a video of the robbery. As you know, his mobile is missing, and according to his mobile provider, the phone's been switched off since last night. No calls in or out from just after 8pm. They're chasing his internet usage for the previous twenty-four hours. Should be with us before tomorrow.'

'I think we know where this is going. The reason he takes nothing is because his true quarry is more personal. I bet, from what you've said, he's settling some crazy, personal score. Revenge is best served cold comes to mind.'

There was a pause as Skeeter looked at Steve. He moved forward on the chair, his interest piqued as Skeeter put the call on speaker.

'It has to be the action, the posting of the video, or the actual act of videoing rather than the person themselves, otherwise how would he know they'd be present? It's random revenge, a kind of roulette.' You could almost hear the thought process in her words.

'Or a staged set,' Skeeter responded. 'It was set up, planned, knowing how many people these days, on seeing incidents like the robberies, immediately pick up their phones and record. I guess in such incidences there would be quite a few. I've seen it and so have you. Add a flashing blue light and you may as well shout, "Lights, Camera, Action!"'

Steve chuckled, nearly expelling the wine he had just sipped.

'Something else. Lucy was looking into past attacks, one in particular where a young woman was killed by two blokes on motorbikes. It was mentioned at the briefing.'

'Yes, eleven months ago,' Skeeter looked across at Steve.

'I am aware that you and Lucy are going to interview the witnesses again. I think you know where my thought process is taking me. The woman killed was someone's daughter, someone's wife and therefore ... I just wonder if someone posted that, too, and it was seen by a loved one. Such an action could possibly make many of us want to seek revenge, maybe even take a life.'

Skeeter let the information sink in before she replied. 'Indeed, April. Now we have a number of the Red Hoods in custody could that be the end?' Skeeter's tone was not convincing.

'Or maybe, as we've thought for a while, just the start or even a build-up to a spectacular ending? Whatever he's planning he's started to sort the wheat from the chaff. I think I need a drink! Anyway, thanks again, and my apologies for disturbing your evening. Please say hi to Steve.' She hung up.

'The guy you found, another victim?'

Skeeter nodded. 'We knew he was linked owing to the hood he was wearing. It could have been some crazy copycat thing until it came to light. As you heard, he also posted the robbery on various social media platforms. It seems to be the common denominator. That's two, possibly three who've made that mistake and they've paid dearly for it.'

'So, from what you say, he sets the scene, watches those people present and …'

'But how does he track them?'

Steve took a sip of his wine. 'I would say for someone in the know that's fairly straight forward. He clicked on the person's video post, then the location tag showing who had posted. It might not reveal their real name. He then looked at the person's interests, friends, photographs. Some people are very accommodating and practically tell you their life history, the type who seek approval, fame in particular. If needs be, he might send a message or a friend request, maybe a message stating it was a great video or asking if they're safe – false praise or playing to their narcissistic nature that they obviously have, to break down barriers. It's amazing just how much you can discover in a short period of time. Then, of course, once you have a name, finding an address is relatively simple. If the site is private, he probably moves on. Remember, it's the act he's probably rebelling against and not the specific person.'

It suddenly seemed so simple.

'We did that with Caitlin Byrne's phone and the request was accepted post death,' Skeeter said in a whisper.

Steve poured more wine. 'You say the robberies were during the working week, so your controller guy appears to have time on his hands. Is he not working, working flexible hours, shifts? He's certainly not holding down a regular nine to five. He's controlling the date and time of the robberies, so it would be easy.'

'There's a maturity in that, to be able to plan well ahead when dealing with six or more foot-soldiers,' Skeeter mused as she sat on the settee, her legs curled beneath her. 'So, let's put a perspective on this from what we already know, or think we know. He's mature, not one of the lads. He has some kind of qualification in IT or a sound working knowledge of technology. He doesn't work or he works irregular hours. He's seeking some kind of revenge. Anything missing?' Skeeter looked across, anticipating something from left field and she wasn't disappointed.

'Just tell me about the hoods.'

She went through their history and briefly mentioned Michael's theory. As she talked, it sounded even more crazy than when she had first heard about it.

'So, the hoods are only a recent prop, and those have evolved. The ones found recently were not made by the lad who admits to making the others?'

Skeeter nodded. 'We'll have to check the one on the body this morning but the one from the metal man, yes.' She wondered where his meandering thoughts were going.

'From where I'm sitting, that's logical, too, then. He makes his own as they never meet him and delivery of any goods is purely one way. Anything else would be too dangerous. To me, and this is purely speculative, to find your controller you should be looking back, as you will be doing with Lucy. Searching for the spark that lit the fire for revenge—'

'But—'

'Just hear me out and then shoot me down in flames. You should determine how the revenge was planned, and hope that you might find critical evidence, as Michael has hypothesised, within the comic book story. Ask yourself is the killer a man who was let down by someone who once cared? Did he not aid when help was needed? Has righting the wrong, the seeking of revenge, been driven by this and more? Did the police not do their job? Did someone video or photograph a tragedy in his life rather than assist? You said the cold case you're reassessing was never solved. Was that videoed?'

Skeeter seemed to recall it had been, but the posts had since been removed. She nodded as if the scales had been falling from her eyes as he spoke. There was a momentary silence, apart from the crackle of the wood burning in the stove. They both sat in the semi-dark, the yellow glow of firelight dancing on every surface, bringing moving shadows and warmth.

'Not just a pretty face, are you, fly boy?' She sidled across and kissed him.

CHAPTER 26

There had been a thick mist that morning, but it was now slowly beginning to dissipate. The air was still heavy, and the sounds exaggerated. Alan Green tugged his black hood up until the front hung like a monk's habit concealing his face. His hands were thrust deep into his pockets as he made his way to his private place, his sanctuary, to the dragon's eye, the only space he knew where he would be safe. He needed time to think. His night had been troubled, and his sleep had been either fitful or non-existent. His mind was saturated and confused as the news had broken that a further body had been found, a body wearing another red hood. There had been no image, but he had created his own and it haunted him. He knew it would only be a matter of time before he heard the crash on his door, and he also knew it would come very late at night or early in the morning, these calls always did. There would be no polite knock. Even so, he knew his mother would try to protect him, offer the alibi he needed. She always had, right from his time in school. She had been a formidable ally, her anger a trait he had inherited, her words often bringing teachers to tears. But then, she should defend him. He had tolerated so much from the many different men who had come down the stairs – the sounds, the laughter, the hunger and often the pain they sometimes brought. He had forgotten what his own father looked like. He was long gone on account of her drinking, drugs and prostitution, although she was always in denial over all three. On more than one occasion, when he was quite young, he had been a victim of a stranger's lust.

Leaning on the broken brick wall, he watched. He was good at that. He was patient and calm. The grey tendrils of the morning's mist seemed lazy and languid, bringing with them a chill. His eyes focused deep into the sparse woodland where the trees' finer lines smudged and blurred. The indistinct shapes brought a fuzziness and a peace and quiet. He waited and watched for any dog walkers who might be out early whilst he inhaled his e-cigarette, the vapour soon camouflaged within the surrounding air. He was in no hurry. He failed, as usual, to form a smoke ring.

The portal, as he called it, was well-hidden and set within an overhang of moss-covered rock. Removing the few stones he had placed when he had last left, he revealed the entrance. Squeezing through the gap he allowed his feet to fall onto the uneven surface and leaned out to replace the stones. The darkness before him was like pitch, thick and all enveloping, but it offered a safety and security the streets at this time did not; it was his friend. His hand groped instinctively until it found the metal rod; it was exactly where he had left it. It was his aid to walking along the uneven passageway; it was also useful as a signal. That role was now obsolete as he was expecting nobody. This place was banned to the others, not that there were many still free. The speed of the roundup had not been a surprise. It was determined by how long tongues would remain still or names and numbers from their personal phones remained undeleted. Tongues had wagged of that, he was sure.

Flicking on his head torch, he made his way through the

passageway towards the chamber that held the eye. He glanced at the red sign on the lintel above, 'Welcome to Hell'. Here, the ceiling was at its lowest point as the ground ran up towards an entrance, his entrance. Soon, it spread to a good height and breadth where the concrete pillars had been placed to secure the broad roof.

Hearing a noise, he paused, dropped low, immediately turning off his light. He listened. The silence, like the blackness, was thick and sticky. It was then that he saw the briefest of flashes. It was needle-sharp, moving from left to right way down the passage to his left. He waited. The noise and the light appeared again; this time, the light remained and bounced as if carried by someone finding the progress difficult. Whoever it might be was moving up the passageway. Green sat on his haunches, his back against one of the geodetic concrete columns that concealed him but allowed him a clear view of the tres-passer. He remained silent. Within seconds the person's form became visible. It was Smigga.

Green carefully lifted his hand to his head torch and switched it back on. The strong beam hit Smigga full in the face.

'Fucking hell, Ahhh!' The involuntary screech echoed and amplified against the stone confines as he stumbled onto one knee, his breathing deep and heavy. 'Who the fuck's there?'

Green tapped the rod on the ground, the signal.

'Greenie? Oh Jesus! You scared the fucking daylights out of me.'

Green stood, said nothing and headed down the passageway to the cavern, sitting where he normally held court. He waited. Within seconds, Smigga stumbled in.

'Took the wrong turn again.'

'Shine your torch at the ceiling. What do you see, Smig?'

Uncertain of the answer he should give, he paused. 'The dragon's eye?'

'The dragon's eye. Correct. And when you were last under the eye, what instructions did I give you? No, it was an order.'

'To bring everything and hide it. Break down the bike, hide the hoods and the phones. We did, if you remember. You saw us.'

'And?' There was a growing anger in his voice, an anger that he could normally control.

'This place would be out of bounds.' His voice shook as he spoke. 'I'm sorry, Greenie. I didn't know where else to go.'

'So why are you fucking here?' He brought the iron rod down onto the side of Smigga's knee. The crack was loud. It was swiftly followed by Smigga's scream.

'Shit!'

'Well? Answer the bloody question or do you want another crack?'

Smigga held up his hand in supplication before removing the small backpack he was carrying. He brought out a blue nylon rope. 'I couldn't cope, Greenie, I couldn't do with being put inside. It wouldn't be a juvenile lock-up now. It'd be for real and fuck I couldn't do that.'

Green's head lamp shone directly into his face, and he could see his distress as he handled the rope.

'Why am I here? I thought I'd go deep into the passage and … well … just end it.'

'But you didn't have the balls to do that, did you? You really are an arse. Why have they given you bail, do you think? Why are you allowed to go home? Because you'll probably be given a suspended sentence you soft twat. The prisons are full. So, what do you do, Smig? You come here when you might be under surveillance. If they can't get you to tell them who else was involved, they release you and monitor your whereabouts. Like a cat with a mouse. It will not be long before my name is mentioned.'

Smigga shook his head. 'I don't think so. The lads are shit

scared of you, especially when you lose it. Christ, I'm sorry. I didn't think.' He burst into tears.

* * *

Lucy had collected the list of the people who had witnessed Kate Nolan's death. She also had the contact details of her next of kin. Whilst reading the witness statements, one in particular stood out, it was that of Nigel Chadburn. He had been within touching distance of her and had witnessed the whole episode. It was clear from what had been said that he had felt a disturbing degree of guilt. It was mentioned in his statement that he had been angered by the people videoing the girl's demise. There were Google Street View images attached showing the path Kate had walked and the exact location of her death.

The second statement to catch her attention came from her work colleague who mentioned Kate had said she had a clandestine meeting on the day she had been killed. Michael had been co-opted to investigate further and had presented a timeline of the tragic day. Looking at the photograph of Kate, she felt the process unnerving. Piecing together the final steps of the young woman made her reflect on a life we take so much for granted. How we never know just what is round the corner. She turned to Skeeter whilst holding a photograph of Kate towards her.

'To think this woman woke that morning and nothing was out of the ordinary. She probably kissed her partner goodbye, went to work, nipped out at lunchtime and never came back. In the blink of an eye her life and her future were stolen, not only for her but for those who loved her, and for what? A bloody handbag!'

'And those responsible for her death, her manslaughter, are still walking the streets.' Skeeter's anger was evident. 'Mark my words, there's something here that's been missed.'

* * *

Nigel Chadburn stood inside an informal incident room. The modern décor was designed to put people at ease, particularly those seeking help and support. It was certainly plush. He nursed a coffee as he inspected the sepia photographs of Liverpool's history, how the city had developed architecturally if not morally. He briefly forgot the reason he was there as a sudden sense of pride flushed through him. The fully glazed wall to one side gave a view over what was once Speke Airport before the runway and the hangars were relocated literally only a stone's throw away.

Lucy and Skeeter entered introducing themselves.

'The new police centre is pretty special, better than the old place in which I was previously interviewed.' His nervousness was obvious.

'We're sorry to have had to ask you to come in, Mr Chadburn, but as you know, we've been having a spate of motorcycle attacks. We would very much like to catch the people whose crime you witnessed.'

He nodded in agreement and looked down at the remnants in the bottom of his coffee cup. 'It was a dreadful moment in time. The guilt I felt was crushing. If you only knew the number of times I've asked myself why I didn't act differently on that day. If only ... if only, seemed to be the two words I couldn't erase from my thoughts. It still haunts me to this day when I see a pedestrian crossing. A different action on my part and things might have been so different. She might still be alive.'

'It wasn't your fault. I believe you had some professional support to overcome that anxiety?' Skeeter asked already knowing the answer. She knew the Police Family Support Team had been involved and counselling had been accepted.

Chadburn nodded. 'I was sceptical when it was first offered

but I quickly became a convert, so much so, I found myself able to attend Kate's funeral. I didn't go into the chapel as there were so many people there and I didn't want to intrude but I paid my respects from outside.' He smiled, the kind of smile that looked as though his lip was about to quiver. 'I thought seeing the people who cared about her, loved her, would be a true test to see if I was conquering my shame and guilt.'

Lucy offered him a smile. 'It obviously worked?'

He did not respond, merely turned to look towards the window.

'I know from your statement that you didn't notice anything significant about the people on the bike. Has anything come to you since? The smallest thing could make all the difference.'

He laughed, it was dry and cynical. 'As you've said, we seem to have more and more of these yobs and neither you nor anyone else appears to be in a position to stop them. Look at the recent attacks, those wearing ridiculous red hoods. Just like Kate's attack, it happens in broad daylight, they plough their way along pavements and all some people can do is video them instead of doing something positive.' He paused as if suddenly remonstrating with himself again. 'I guess I've no room to talk. What did I do?'

'More to the point, Mr Chadburn, what could you have done? These things happen so quickly. No one is prepared. And now with the knife crime—'

'Do you think you'll ever catch those who attacked her?'

Skeeter looked at Lucy wondering how she might answer.

'They all look the same, the bikes, the clothing. Many are just kids, too. Catch them for that particular crime?' Lucy shook her head. 'Unless someone confesses or someone offers a piece of definitive evidence on which we can act, I doubt it.'

By late afternoon, Lucy and Skeeter had interviewed all the

key witnesses. They had drawn the same conclusion as the initial investigation. They planned to have a late lunch before the final interview. Rob Duncan, Kate's work colleague, had requested the interview take place in his office, citing work commitments.

CHAPTER 27

The office block was relatively modern, and yet the process of arriving and meeting the person they had come to see at the specified location seemed plagued with bureaucracy. The internal communication system was clearly locked in the past. Lucy and Skeeter were held at various stages of their progress by an overbearing receptionist who kept checking the time, smiling and returning to her computer screen.

'I could happily put her in a half nelson until she cried,' Skeeter whispered. 'It's as if she has a bad smell permanently under her nose.'

Lucy laughed, causing the receptionist to peer over her glasses.

'Oops!'

'Don't poke the bear!' Skeeter giggled.

It was twenty minutes later when they were finally directed down a long corridor. A large door opened and the man they had come to see appeared.

'Duncan, Rob Duncan. I'm so sorry for the delay but one can never plan to the minute as I'm sure you're well aware in your vital work. A late phone call from across the pond. Come in and have a seat. Again, my apologies. I wasn't expecting two of you but you're welcome. How may I help?'

Lucy went through the line of enquiry as Skeeter made notes.

'That's what she said, Detective, they were her exact words: "a clandestine meeting". Knowing her as I did, I believed it to be said in jest. In fact, I laughed when she came out with it. Kate had a wonderful sense of humour. It was only after her cruel death that it seemed to take on a more sinister connotation. As a lawyer, where interpretation of the spoken and written word is critical, I had some concerns and, therefore, I could understand the confusion it brought to Tim Foxton and to the police as we had, at the time, nothing to determine her true meaning. However, as you now know, it all became clear. She was planning a surprise holiday for her partner. The clandestine meeting was with a travel agent and not a secret agent or worse.' He smiled but quickly let it fall from his lips on seeing Skeeter's disapproval. 'Sorry, yes. Bad taste.'

'You attended the funeral?' Skeeter immediately asked.

'Of course, she was a valued colleague and a friend. We'd known each other for some time. I invited her to work here knowing her strict and dedicated work ethic. The funeral, I'm pleased to say, was well attended. She was a lovely lady. It was a tragedy what happened to her. Such a waste. Wouldn't we all like to get our hands on the mindless yobs who caused her death?'

Skeeter looked directly at him even though she knew the question was clearly rhetorical. Neither did they answer, but Lucy immediately embarked onto a different tack.

'This might be a difficult question, Mr Duncan, but could you tell me about your personal relationship with Ms Nolan?'

Rob Duncan moved uncomfortably on his chair but quickly recovered his composure. 'Was it so obvious?'

'We've made enquiries,' Skeeter snapped, keeping him more on tenterhooks.

'Her mother, no doubt. Anyway, before she met Tim Foxton, we were close.'

Lucy said nothing but paused, hoping he would say more. She did not have to wait long.

'At that time, the relationship with my partner was fraught, brought about by the death of her son. I suppose, as we'd lived together for over eighteen months, you could say he was my stepson.'

He shifted his body in the chair again as if uncertain whether he should dredge up the past.

'I'm sorry to hear that, my condolences.' Lucy frowned.

'Thanks. The lad and I got on well as we got to know each other. It was difficult as Penny had experienced a few relationships before we met, so he'd had men in his life as he was growing up. Although it was difficult at first, as I settled in, the situation became more comfortable. The older he got, the more the barriers disappeared. I'd like to believe we enjoyed each other's company.'

'How old was he, Mr Duncan?'

'Fourteen. He was a back seat passenger with two other teenagers in his friend's father's car. The driver was the older brother of his best mate, who was also in the car. It was taken without their parents' permission, which made things worse. They'd been to a football match. It was winter and dark when they were heading home. Witnesses said the car was speeding. They didn't all survive the crash. The car hit a wall before turning over into a flooded ditch. All but one managed to free themselves. Stephen was the only fatality.' He took a deep breath as if to rally himself. 'Anyway, Penny went to pieces, she was sectioned twice as she attempted suicide, once very publicly. I tried to help but I couldn't. She blamed me, and in some ways, if you look at it fatalistically, she was right. I'd given him permission to go. Unbeknown to me at the time, she'd refused him. If I'd said no, he'd still be here, and we might still be together. So, as you can imagine, living with her, trying to support her when I was to her the guilty party, just became impossible. In her eyes I'd killed him. I tried, believe me, I tried.'

Lucy said nothing but felt his grief. Skeeter looked directly at him, sceptical about his sincerity.

'I moved into a flat. There was no hope of our staying together. So, to get to your question, Kate had been a friend of a friend, and she saw I was wounded. In reality, I was emotionally destroyed. I didn't know how to handle the guilt I felt. I needed a shoulder, someone to share my trauma, then one thing led to another. To be honest, I wasn't ready for another relationship and, intuitively, she could sense that. She saw it was going nowhere, but she stayed longer than she should. I was grateful for her love and support. Anyway, we agreed she should have a break, take a holiday. She went away with some girlfriends, and it was when she was there that she met Tim, who, strangely enough, lived here in Liverpool. Our relationship, if you could call it that, had ended, but I was proud to say our friendship continued. In fact, you could say, it deepened. It was purely platonic and had been for some time.'

'Did you know Stephen's father?' Skeeter asked.

Rob Duncan shook his head. 'Never, I didn't even try to approach him. All I knew was that he was some kind of doctor. Penny refused to mention him or talk about their relationship, if that's what you could call it. From what I understood, it might have been a one-night stand, but that could be apocryphal, my misplaced interpretation. I believe she became pregnant not long after they'd met, and he buggered off on hearing the news. I don't believe I will ever know the truth. I don't think they ever lived together, and if they did, it wasn't for long. One thing I do know for sure, he didn't come to the funeral and if he did, he was outside. Penny would have said if he had, she'd have probably exploded. It was held at Anfield cemetery. Even the sky cried that day.'

'I'm sorry, Mr Duncan. I know it's not been easy for you but thank you for sharing that.' Skeeter and Lucy stood. 'We've taken too much of your time and thank you for your honesty.'

'Aren't you going to ask me about Penny?' He stood, straightened the knot of his tie and leaned forward on the desk as if to steady himself. Lucy flushed, it was her turn to feel uncomfortable, but Skeeter folded her arms as if to form a barrier and waited for him to continue.

* * *

'For fuck's sake Smigga, stop snivelling and grow the fuck up. You've been a bad lad, but you've only snatched from a few people and robbed a couple of shops. It's not as if you've killed anyone. Is it the woman's death? Is that what's given you Sparra's Grobbelaar legs?'

Smigga wiped his face on his sleeve and took a deep breath. 'Is it true what Micky says?'

'What the fuck are you on about? What's he been saying?'

'He told me a while back that you killed a woman. You didn't mean to kill her, it just happened like, an accident. Is it true or was he winding me up like he does all the time?'

A silence prevailed as if the surrounding darkness had sucked away the air and any sounds. The light shining directly from Green's head torch made him blind to his swiftly changing expression. 'What did he say, Smigga?'

'Not much really as he was pissed. Something about he'd grabbed her bag, and she'd hung on but then she'd let go as you sped away. As she fell, she went under a truck or something. He said, Greenie, he said …' there was a pause that seemed to hang in the darkness. '… He'd kill me if I told anyone. He told me you were driving. He also said you didn't know she'd died until later. You'd just fucked off, like, with the bag and hadn't seen what happened to her. So, I said to Micky that you didn't really kill her, but Micky says that the Bizzies wouldn't think that. He said had she not held on to her bag she'd … I've told no one, Greenie, honest.'

'You've told me, Smig, you've told me and I'm not no one … You gobshite.'

The silence returned, claustrophobic and menacing. Smigga could feel the pulse of his heart in his ears, it was fast and pounding, as if counting time. The light was still blinding. Green lifted his hand and turned off his head torch and the cavern blackness drained them both of their senses as Smigga fumbled blindly for his lamp.

* * *

'Penny? She moved away, started, I can only assume, a new life away from Merseyside. I never heard from her again, not a dickie bird. But then, why should I have? I thought if she heard the news about Kate she might reach out.' He laughed to himself and raised both his eyebrows and hands. 'Maybe I didn't know her as well as I thought.' He looked at his watch. 'Sorry, but that's it, unless you've a surprise up your sleeves!' He looked straight at Skeeter, his mood immediately changing.

She shook her head. 'You've been most helpful. Thank you.'

'Why are you looking back at this case? Is it because of the bike gangs?'

'We have two, maybe three murders, all linked to some of the robberies. People who posted videos of the attacks have been found murdered. It's been on the news and in the press.'

'I saw that, yes. And for those murders to happen, revenge must have played a key part? I suppose with my legal hat on you're looking to find the spark that brought the fire? Could that have been Kate's untimely death?'

Lucy was momentarily taken aback. She could only nod.

'Do you know anything else?' Skeeter asked, fixing him with a stare.

'Sorry but I can offer you little more. As I said, I do have a lot of work to do.' His smile was false but not vindictive.

'One last question if I may,' Skeeter continued as she turned to leave. 'Do you know, or have you ever known, where Stephen's father lived?'

A shake of the head answered her question. 'I never did, and I had no intention of ever finding out. Knowing the calibre of the man, a man I despised. I can assure you I have even less interest to do so now, sorry.'

The pavement was busy as they left the front entrance to the block. It had been disconcerting just how little they had known about him until then and their curiosity had been sparked.

There was an industrious hum as they entered the Incident Room. Lucy tossed her coat and bag on to a chair before propping her backside on a desk as Skeeter found a chair.

'Penny for them,' Phil Lipson asked, looking at each colleague in turn.

'Some people have tragedy in their lives and manage to carry on, make something of themselves, and yet others just crumble. I wonder if revenge comes from resentment, impotence, anger or none of those,' Lucy answered.

Phil typed the word into Google. 'Here you go, Lucy. Revenge according to the fount of all knowledge: "Harm done to someone for harm that they have done to someone else", or you could have "Retaliation in kind or degree".' He grinned, looking up from the screen. 'What did we do before the internet?'

It was Skeeter who answered. 'Some people might still be alive. Social media is the devil's work.' She sat and added the notes she had made into the computer.

* * *

'Put the fucking light on, Greenie, don't piss abou—' Smigga did not finish the sentence. The iron bar crashed down, skimming the right side of his head before travelling to his shoulder and collar bone. There followed a loud expulsion of air, bringing with it a deep, guttural gurgle and the muffled thud as his body collapsed forward.

As the light returned, Smigga's body was slumped rag-doll-like as if in prayer. 'You fucking gobshite. Just how many people have you bloody well told?' Green looked up at the ceiling. The giant eye stared back. His thoughts now turned to Micky Webster, and the immediate black turned to red mist. He allowed himself another kick at the prostrate figure before collecting Smigga's torch. 'Micky should have kept you in the fucking dark.' He threw the torch against the stone wall and the shattering sound reverberated within the huge, hollow space. 'If you fucking wake up, let's see if you can find your way out in the total blackness. As sure as eggs are eggs, you struggle with a torch, so you'll need a fair degree of fucking luck.' The headlamp focused on the blood that was seeping from the large gash just above Smigga's ear. 'We'd sworn a vow of silence, like blood brothers do. I didn't break that promise. I honoured our vows. He'll pay, Smigga, on that you can bet your life.'

CHAPTER 28

Alan Green paused at the gate to his house. It sat centrally within a row of three. The front garden was a mess, it was always a mess. Domestic rubbish locked within the weeds and grass having been abandoned there for as long as he could remember. The living room window was almost opaque as the trapped condensation within the fractured double-glazed unit grew like a hazy bloom. The curtains offered nothing in terms of a welcome as they hung at an angle. The words 'shit' and 'house' came to his mind and not for the first time. Turning the key, he entered. The stench of tobacco and fried food briefly stung his eyes; it was ever thus. The living room was a jumble, the large flat-screen television attached to the chimney breast dominated the room. It was always on, the sound low. That screen, too, was not straight and the wires dangled beneath diagonally to a plug on the side wall like entrails. Seeing the number of empty beer cans scattered on the top of the coffee table warned him of what was happening.

He paused, taking in what, to him, was now the norm – the chaos accompanied by a cacophony of familiar noises. They drifted down from upstairs, they were the animalistic accompaniment associated with rough sex. He could even discern his mother's grunts and groans above the regular noise of the heaving bed. Moving through to the kitchen, another area of chaos, he opened the fridge, grabbed a beer, the only one that remained, and returned to sit on the chair in the living room. Kicking off the cans, he lifted his feet and rested them on the coffee table. Within minutes, the noise from upstairs subsided, and, thankfully, came to a halt. He knew, whoever it might be, would now be having a fag. They would soon be down. If the usual pattern were followed, the bloke would either have another beer or just pay and bugger off. Holding the last can, he knew today it would be the latter. The collective laughter threw him off guard. He could discern two male voices along with the high-pitched laughter of his mother. He sighed. It was still only 11.30. These were probably the first visitors of the day, but he knew from experience, they would unlikely be the last.

'Shit hole,' he said to himself. 'A fucking brothel and a shit hole.' He sipped from the can, awaiting the arrival of the clients from the upstairs room. He did not have to wait long as the first man appeared. He was elderly, and from the colour of his skin, certainly not English. He glanced round the door, nodded and left before the second came down the stairs. He was younger and loitered in the doorway and grinned.

'You must be next in line, la'. We've warmed her up for ya.'

His lewd grin brought the half empty beer can close to his head. It bounced off the wall behind him before landing on the lino, spinning and fizzing like a Catherine wheel. The foaming beer splattered the man's trousers as well as the wall and door.

'Fuck off now, you mucky old bastard before I fucking cool you down once and for all. I'm her son and I'm certainly not in the fucking mood to listen to you.'

Alan kicked over the coffee table in his effort to get to his feet and to the man, who took seconds to find the door handle and escape. Alan collected the can and threw it after him. As he slammed the door he heard the toilet flush; he turned to see his mother coming down the stairs, her dressing gown wrapped around her, the remains of the cigarette still between her lips.

'Hello, love. See 'em off did you? I need a brew. Want one?'

He followed her into the kitchen. 'Why can't we have a real house, a home, a decent life like other families do?'

She let the cigarette drop from her lips into the sink, turned on the tap before forcing the remnants down the drain with her finger.

'We do, love. Pass that packet of sugar. That's why I'm looking after you and making this brew. It's what mothers do.'

'Who were they then. Uncle Sid and Uncle Brian? Are you going to tell me the same lies you did when I was a nipper and then fob me off with a few quid? You really can't believe this shit house is normal? Look at it for fuck's sake!'

She turned, removed the fags from her pocket and lit another on the gas stove. She just pulled a face suggesting she did not understand what all the fuss was about.

'You've never been a real mum nor a wife. The booze, the drugs and any excuse to get a shag have always been more important to you than a home or a real family. You're nothing but a whore, that's what Dad called you, that's why he left.' Alan slammed his fist into the wall.

'I've always stuck up for you, fought your battles, been with you when the shit hit the fan, shit of your own making. It didn't matter if you were right or wrong, I still stood by you. That's what mothers do. They protect their offspring no matter what. You've turned out alright.'

Alan shook his head. 'Protect me? You turned a blind eye when your men friends abused me as a nipper when you were incapable of satisfying them because you were off your head.'

'You never told me that before.' For the first time he

witnessed a genuine look of concern on her face. 'I didn't know that, love. Why didn't you say anything? You want that brew?'

'I did, but you quickly chose to ignore it all. There's something else you don't know.' He paused as she stirred her mug. What little sincerity she showed quickly evaporated. 'I've killed someone.'

Her mouthed dropped. 'What? Don't be so bloody daft.'

'It was some time ago. It was an accident, but it was our fault. The Bizzies don't know it was me, but they could find out soon enough as some of the lads are in custody, one in particular. He was pillion and he grabbed the woman's bag. If he says anything, I'm fucked.'

'I'll say you were here like I've always done. Like I said, son, I protect you.' She moved over to him, her arms spread. Alan moved away.

'I need to disappear. I'll have some cash soon, it's been promised to me, and then I'm gone.'

She moved over to a cluttered work surface, lifted the lid off the teapot and withdrew some cash. 'Take this. It's not much but it shows I love you.'

'You don't know the meaning of the word.'

He threw the money on the floor, ran upstairs, collected some items and a bag and left.

CHAPTER 29

Lucy could see April was free and went straight in.

'It's amazing what you discover when you lift a stone.'

April pointed to the chair. She went through the details taken from the interviews, in another attempt to place the information she had in some sort of order. 'There's something that makes me feel uncomfortable about both these men. Chadburn witnessed it all, a chap minding his own business but who totally lost it after watching Kate's death. So much so that he actually physically attacked someone, we don't know who that was as no complaint was ever made by the victim. He admits to snatching a man's phone and throwing it to the floor. He was also racked with guilt. Counselling was offered and accepted, and if appearances are anything to go by, he seems to have overcome the trauma.'

'Skeeter was in on the interview, and we discussed it afterwards. She feels he was an innocent, just caught up in the chaos and responded totally out of character.' Lucy added.

'She's probably right. Anyway, the solicitor, Rob Duncan, Kate's boss at the time of her death, had an affair with her some while back. Interestingly, before he met her, his life had been beset with distressing situations, too. That troubling time was the reason they came together. He lost a child, his stepson even though he had only lived with the child's mother a short time. The lad died as a result of a car crash in which he was a passenger. Four teenagers were in it, three escaped. Stephen was in the back. His legs were trapped by a seat and as the car was upside down in a flooded ditch, he drowned. If you read the report, Skeeter added it to HOLMES, it might make more sense. I've found this.' She pushed a copy of a news cutting across the table. 'Stephen Melville, fourteen years old.'

The photograph showed a semi-submerged vehicle. The emergency services were clearly seen extracting a body.

'Whoever printed that needs reprimanding.' April frowned, handing back the cutting.

'You can imagine the anger and upset that caused the child's loved ones. Penny Melville tried to take her own life on more than one occasion. Even though she was racked with guilt, she blamed Rob Duncan as he'd allowed the lad to go in the car to a football match. Unbeknown to him at the time, she'd refused Stephen's request.'

April let out a low whistle and shook her head. 'A parenting faux pas. Where is she now?'

It was Lucy's turn to shake her head. 'She packed up and left. Name change? Probably. Married again? Not sure about that as she had been seriously hurt by two men. You know how easy it is to disappear.'

'The father of the child?'

'They weren't married, and, according to Duncan, he buggered off when he knew she was expecting. He came into the relationship when the child was about twelve. According to the copy of the birth certificate,' she pushed it towards April, 'no father's name was added, and this, the death certificate, only confirms that. I've checked the address included in both. It was a house belonging to her parents. They are both dead and the house was sold not long after the child's death. She had no other siblings.'

'I wonder if our mystery man is a woman?' April allowed her fingers to tap the desk.

'That's a thought we had on driving in. A woman scorned. Any news on the CCTV from the pub where Caitlin met her admirer?'

'I'll chase it,' April offered.

'One last thought. We have the River of Light Festival in a couple of days. I take it the bosses on high have arranged some extra plain clothes foot-soldiers as well as regular patrols to be about? The last thing we need is a herd of electric bikes on the snatch as there'll be cameras a-plenty snapping the exhibits.'

'Interesting collective noun, Lucy. Skeeter's been pushing that. I believe they'll have facial recognition in operation around the Pier Head and the Albert Dock. I'm due to have a further planning meeting tomorrow. Good luck this afternoon. Will Skeeter be with you?'

'She wouldn't miss it for the world.'

* * *

Alan Green stared at the Palm House, a huge glass building. He had seen it many times before, but he had never been inside. It was busy, and, the crowd of people offered a degree of anonymity he now craved. Once inside, he found a bench. The warmth seemed reassuring, and for the first time that day, he felt his body relax. Not for long though, as the image of Smigga flooded back, bringing with it a nauseating wave of guilt. He was a mate, they had known each other since primary school. Standing, he went to the door as his eye caught the bronze statue of Peter Pan. His grandad had brought him here for a picnic once – sunshine, jam butties and pop. Pausing, he looked at the finely carved animals set within the bronze base. It was just one of the few happy memories he could recall as a kid. As if by instinct he turned, almost expecting the old man to be watching over him. *It wasn't all bad*, he thought as he began to jog out of the park.

* * *

Rooting in his bag he located his head torch and paused before the entrance to the dragon cave: the stones were not as he had left them. He climbed in and immediately called out Smigga's name. As the sound travelled, it seemed to distort and bounce back, but there was no response. Within minutes, he was under the dragon's eye. Smigga was no longer there. Kneeling, he could see the dried blood; it looked almost black under the sharp, white light.

'Smigga. Stop pissing about!'

He waited, hoping to pick up the slightest of noises, but he heard nothing. The rod Alan had carried was no longer there. Could he have found his way out? If he were honest, he felt relief that he was not still slumped over. He knew the force of the blow and the consequences if it had caught him full on the head; without doubt it would have killed him and one death on his conscience was enough. Alan walked slowly back along the passageway the way he had come, searching for any clues. At the crossroads he turned down the passage that always confused Smigga. He called again and listened. There was no reply.

* * *

The responses Lucy received from Tim Foxton were not what she had expected. He emanated a certain confidence, a disconcerting touch of arrogance but no guilt. Skeeter felt uncomfortable from the beginning. He seemed overly nervous.

'I went through the wringer, especially when the so-called secrets came to light, what she'd said to her boss and the secret cash, the winnings. My despair was doubled. I thought I knew the person with whom I'd been living, the woman I loved. Then you hear and read things and she's gone so you can't question anything. Then come the doubts, the uncertainties begin to gnaw at you. They were real and I was truly angry. Then, of course, I discovered the truth, and so you can guess how that made me feel. It was a roller coaster ride I wouldn't want my worst enemy to go through. I'd just got vaguely sorted and someone mentioned the death had been recorded by some arse. Sorry, but that's the only term they deserve. Apparently, they posted it on some social media platform. It didn't stay on long, but if I'm honest and if I could have found them, I'd have happily taken their life.' He paused, not letting his gaze leave Lucy. 'Is that wrong?'

Lucy thought for a moment, recalling the saying about walking in other people's shoes before passing judgement. She looked briefly at Skeeter before answering. 'I couldn't possibly say but I can fully understand the strength of your feelings at that point. How was your relationship with her boss, Robert Duncan?'

The question brought a short laugh and a shake of his head. 'He gave an accurate interview to you people. What she said was what she said. I might have interpreted it the same way, after all, we both knew Kate, let's just say, we knew her well. Let's also take a moment to remember that the death of a loved one does strange things to you. The death of a parent is in many ways different, still very distressing but in some sense expected, but your lover, your wife or husband, or even a child, is not the same, especially when that death is so unexpected. I looked for someone to blame, and rarely did I allow that focus to fall on myself. I read somewhere that you soul search, dig for reasons or answers. Kate normally didn't work Saturdays, but there was pressure from work for her to do so on that day. If she hadn't gone in … if, if, if, if.' He tripped the words quickly off his tongue as if he had done it many times before. He studied them each in turn. 'That's how my mind was working. I couldn't find an answer because, as I know now, there wasn't one.'

Lucy immediately thought of the remorse and angst demonstrated by Nigel Chadburn. She scribbled a note:

When does remorse stop and revenge begin?

'How are you now, Mr Foxton?'

As the words were uttered, she instantly regretted the question. Skeeter looked directly at him curious as to his response.

He raised his eyebrows. 'I'm trying to sell the flat. Too many memories. I'm still attempting to come to terms with it all. I'm working hard to keep a job for which I now have little enthusiasm, and I'm wondering when you people will be able to do your job and catch the bastards who took Kate's life for the sake of a handbag. That's how I am now!'

His answer reassured Skeeter.

* * *

On returning to the station, Skeeter and Lucy popped their heads round April's door as Skeeter wiped imaginary sweat from her brow.

'How was the interview?'

'That was one angry man. He'd heard about the video that was posted of her death and openly admitted that if he knew the name of the culprit, he'd have killed him. Just like Chadburn, he was full of ifs and no buts. If this hadn't have happened … He had a string of them. I'll chat later, we're gagging for a brew. You?'

April shook her head. 'Before you do. The CCTV from the pub.'

Skeeter and Lucy turned back. 'Is there anything?'

'Digital Forensics have noted a reflection in one of the mirrors. It's not the best image but they assure me it's nobody we've questioned and nobody on file.'

'Have Chadburn and Foxton been checked against it?' Skeeter asked.

'It's drawn a blank. However, here it is.'

They looked at the large screen behind them. The face was indistinct. 'He's wearing a tie,' Skeeter announced.

April stood next to her.

'There, it's visible. Clean shaven. I'm seeing a man of a certain age. A professional?'

'Works flexible hours or doesn't work at all. I think it was you who added that idea.' April went to the computer. 'Here it is,' She brought up the file and read it. '"He could be working flexible hours, shifts. He's certainly not holding down a regular nine to five as he's controlling the date and time."'

'It was Steve who thought about that if I'm honest,' Skeeter admitted.

'It's certainly logical.'

CHAPTER 30

Michael Peet had not slept well. There was something nagging at him, and although he had jotted notes on the pad next to his bed when the thoughts came to him, it meant he had slept fitfully. At two in the afternoon, he climbed out of bed, made a coffee and sat in front of his computer. Looking at his notes, he typed into Google, 'Batman Film', 'Liverpool' and was immediately rewarded by a string of relevant results. One in particular caught his eye, a post in the *Liverpool Echo*. It included the trailer for the film. He ran it, his finger hovering in readiness to pause when a location he knew came into view. The night time emotive shot of a misty Liver Building clock was the first followed by St George's Hall. Neither location seemed relevant to the case. Scrolling down, he read the article fully. Pausing halfway through, he read it again. A flutter of excitement caused him to smile. Sitting back, he collected his coffee and took a sip, it was now lukewarm. On reading the words, 'Anfield Cemetery', he knew immediately he had found a link, and he understood the relevance. Googling more specifically, a photograph emerged of the actor playing Batman astride a black motorcycle at the cemetery gates. He read the article out loud.

'"Anfield Cemetery had been selected as the perfect location owing to its gothic architectural style. It was felt it epitomised Gotham City. The magnificent wrought iron gates set within the grotesque and sinister stone gates on Cherry Lane, were not only in keeping with the mood and atmosphere of the film but also the vision of the fictitious city in which it is set."'

Moving quickly to Google Maps and Street View, he located the site. It was not the regular entrance to the cemetery, nor was it the magnificent gothic tower between the gates to the south west entrance. He picked up his phone.

'Skeeter, it's Michael. I know, I know, you believe I'm nocturnal but ...'

'You couldn't sleep. Were the kids too noisy?'

'Bloody work, and, in particular, this murder case has hijacked my circadian rhythm. My Batman theory, Red Hood and Robin will not stop churning my head to mush.'

Skeeter swung back on her chair. 'I'm all ears, Michael.'

'Did you know Liverpool was used as a location during the making of a Batman movie back in about 2022?'

'Strangely, and this might sound out of character, I didn't, but I'm willing to learn more.'

'They chose select locations owing to their gothic or sinister architectural style. As you probably know, that's how Gotham City is portrayed in the comics and films. Anyway, some of the locations used held little to no relevance to the case, but one did, the gates to the cemetery on Cherry Lane. That's not all. How is Batman portrayed in that scene?'

'Can I phone a friend? Not a clue.'

'He was astride a black motorcycle. Something else, there's a shot where there are two bikes appearing from the darkness of the arched gateway.'

'So why is that relevant other than the bikes? I can appreciate your cotton-thin link there but it's not telling me anything. What am I missing?'

'If my memory is correct, Kate Nolan was cremated at that cemetery.'

'As are thousands of others, Michael.'

'They were all murdered, too, were they?' He paused allowing the relevance to sink in. 'Skeeter, the film is about vengeance. Imagine if you'd been driven past the gates of the cemetery with its gothic clock tower, and your loved one was in a box in the back, if you had stared at those sinister gates, if you were looking for answers because her killers were still free? Now imagine if he knew something about the comic book characters and knew about the film and the setting, if he knew all about Red Hood, if at the same time he had the fire of anger raging within ...'

Immediately, Skeeter thought of the recent conversation she had held with Tim Foxton. 'Loads of ifs but not buts,' she said out loud. 'Sorry, Michael, that was a verbal thought. I'm not long back from an interview with Tim Foxton, the very man of whom you speak. Lucy and I interviewed him today. He was just that, a man full of ifs. If Kate had not done this, not done that, she'd still be alive. There was clear inner anger there. Knowing the hurt death brings, we asked ourselves, was he capable of killing?'

Michael came straight back. 'I don't believe it's Foxton. The nag in my stomach grows ever stronger the more I discover. It's to do with vengeance, anger but aimed against someone who has exposed what should never have been exposed. The film, and the idea set within the film, the storyline, is purely one of the keys to the case. Batman was put out on film, demonstrating the full process of evil and the revenge that results from it. The fact that it's set here and around us, the motorbikes, here's a thought: did our killer co-opt the gang purely because of that scene? Remember, the killer, like the film's main character, Batman, remains anonymous but is controlling and effective. The killer for whom we search is also controlling. He gets people to do his bidding and yet receives nothing apart from his next victim on a plate and the bikers have no idea they are being used as a means to an end.'

'So why the hoods, Michael? How do they fit into this theory of yours?'

'They are tags, Skeeter. It's my belief he's not a serial killer in the true sense of the word. We studied them in our training, remember? A serial killer is classed as someone who kills three or more people in a period longer than a month. There is a "cooling off" period between each killing. They often lack empathy or guilt. They also kill for pleasure. I read somewhere that they often employ a mask of sanity to disguise their real psychopathic traits and therefore appear normal, in many cases, even charming.'

Skeeter immediately thought of Foxton.

'This type is not the person for whom we search. Our killer does not meet the criteria. He seeks vengeance. With this kind of killing, there's often regret and a fear, not of being caught but that it will not abate, and so they might need to kill again. They also find that they can't commit their atrocious act – or in some cases acts – in a vacuum, there has to be a way of demonstrating to the world their display of anger, to let people know they're there and to signal that they tag the deaths in such a way as if to say: "it's me again. I'm still about and I need help, I'm so angry." Sometimes the flag they raise is too subtle and they stop, hence the many unsolved killings that remain on the books. The killer returns to their normal ways. Their anger is purged.'

'You've had a restless night! Remember, there's no such thing as a perfect murder, especially today with the development in forensic technology. Do go on.' Skeeter was fascinated.

'Tell me about it. I personally believe the killer is developing the ideas as he goes along. He's planning on the hoof. The method has been designed from his knowledge of the comic books, probably knowledge gained in the innocence of youth. The first victim, we believe, Ghulam, his body was never found, and that must have brought a degree of hurt. He possibly hadn't raised the metaphorical flag high enough. With the second victim, he didn't make that mistake, but he failed to link the hood directly to the victim. He quickly compensated for that by leaving it at Crosby Beach. The third death shows he's got his act together. He now knows what he's doing. He's even brazened enough to kill in the open, in a public space. However, things will change because the bike gang has been dismantled. Whether that was deliberate on his part by setting them too difficult a task, could be debated.'

'He set the challenge too high, or has he had enough?' She did not sound as optimistic as she had hoped. It brought a laugh from them both.

'Possibly the challenge was too great but, yes, also having had enough? Somehow, Skeeter, I don't think so. I suggest we put out a TV and radio appeal, that we show those flags the killer has flown. The hoods, the deaths, a description of the person we believe it to be, a link with Batman and the cemetery gates. It just needs someone to connect two or more of those and we might receive the help we need.'

'Leave it with me and I'll let you know as soon as. Try to get some sleep.'

* * *

Smigga sat on the settee at home, a Pot Noodle in his good hand. He balanced the container between his knees whilst his mother bathed the wound.

'That needs stitches, Matthew. It's very deep. Where did you say that you fell, love?'

'I've told you. I fell off the back of Greenie's bike. It was an accident. I wasn't holding on. It'll be alright. I think this bone here is broken though.' He pointed to his shoulder.

'Green. He got you arrested in the first place. I've told you. Keep well away from him. He'll be the death of you, my lad.'

Matthew nodded. 'Sorry!'

'I've asked Jim from The Crescent to take you to A&E, just to get it checked. You need a tetanus, too. That bone, it's your collar bone, it looks broken to me, and I know it won't heal by itself. He'll just drop you as he's on lates.'

A&E was busy. His mother had zipped up his jacket trapping his arm within to restrict his movement; the empty sleeve dangled and flopped. His limp, his badly bruised face and the floppy sleeve invited a number of curious stares from the bored patients sat waiting. He registered and went to sit down. He had not been there twenty minutes when two police officers entered and went immediately to the reception desk. He instinctively lowered his head in expectation. He did not have long to wait.

'Matthew Smith?'

Smigga looked up at the officer standing before him who just tilted his head towards the reception area. 'A minute. Over here, lad.'

He immediately stood. The officer smiled.

'Thank you. Good news. You've been fast tracked. The nurse will see you immediately. The bad news, however, is that I'll be in attendance but I'm hoping that's okay with you.'

Smigga could only smile. The area was full of small cubicles and a number of nurses and doctors moved quickly between them and the nurses' station positioned away from one wall. Matthew was quickly directed into a cubicle at the far end of the room. He limped over and sat on the gurney as directed, his good arm securing his other at the elbow. The officer stood by the opening until a nurse arrived.

'Been in the wars, Matthew?' he asked without an ounce of sympathy as a nurse entered.

'Matthew?' She went through his personal details. 'What have you been up to?'

He looked at the officer and then the nurse. 'A fall.'

'That's not from a fall.' She looked him straight in the eyes. 'I need to know the truth to be able to treat the wound appropriately. The collar bone is broken, I don't need an x-ray to tell me, but you'll still be having one.'

'It was a metal bar. I was accidentally hit when we were messing about.'

'And the limp? Please let me see the leg. Drop your jeans.'

She helped with the belt, button and zip. The knee was heavily swollen and the deep, colourful bruising ran all the way down his calf.

'And this, Matthew? What caused this?'

'I'd rather not say. I'll leave if you can't help. I wouldn't have come only my mum said I'd need a tetanus. I don't like pricks.'

The nurse looked at the officer who fought to keep a straight face. Shrugging her shoulders, she left the cubicle. Within half an hour, the wound had been stitched, and it was confirmed the collar bone was indeed broken.

'It will take about six weeks to heal fully, Matthew. The sling will keep the arm in position. There's a leaflet here along with some painkillers. You need to rest as much as possible. The sutures will dissolve in time. If you start to get headaches or dizziness, come straight back. According to the x-ray, there's no cranial damage.' She touched his arm. 'I think the officers will be taking you home.'

* * *

Alan Green crossed the road in front of the Adelphi Hotel and glanced up at the bronze, naked figure standing on the bow of a ship with all on display, set on the corner of the building opposite. It brought a smile. *Didn't think it was that cold, mister!* he thought as he focused his attention on an exposed part of the man's anatomy. The sound of a car's horn made him jump and move quickly away. He had come off track to be here. For the next night or two he would be in the dragon's cave, and he needed to make provision.

He kept to the left when walking down Ranelagh Street and entered Go Outdoors. Within twenty minutes, he had bought a waterproof sleeping bag, a flask, another headtorch and a rucksack. He needed to buy food and to kill as much time as possible before heading to his sanctuary.

CHAPTER 31

The brown mud and sand sparkled as it lipped the sun-bathed island a short distance away. The twin docks, cut square into the land, held two moored tankers that had arrived the previous day. The sailors looked like small ants as they worked along the side of the dock. The River Mersey, on this bright day, was a deep sepia colour, visible only by the swirls and irregular lines and folds that marked its broad surface. It seemed full of hidden movement, and yet, to the casual observer, it appeared flat, safe and calm. It was in direct contrast to the dark water of the Manchester Ship Canal, it was full of ripples as the breeze channelled down the narrow waterway. The curious onlooker moved his hand to the knot of his tie, making fine adjustments using the reflection in the huge window. He felt, for the first time in a long time, without a worry or a care. It was as if the sun had finally broken through the thick quilt of cloud, stripping away the darkness that had lingered for far too long.

Returning to his desk, he unlocked the drawer before removing the phones; each was different in age and style, each held a memory, a memory that was somehow alien and unreal.

He stared at the cover of the comic; the character wearing the red hood stared back. It no longer seemed to speak to him. Removing the news cuttings, he looked at the photograph of the submerged vehicle and wondered what his life might have been like had the car managed to negotiate the corner at speed, had been driven more slowly, had the driver dropped Stephen at home. What he did know was that four people would still be alive.

'It was not my fault.' His words filled the empty office.

Flicking through the comic, his mind drifted from the present to the past. He remembered the night, the party. She had looked so beautiful. He knew he loved her from that moment but then had come the taunts. *How do you know the child in me is yours?* If truth be told, he did not, what with her reputation. Daddy supported her, spoiled her. It was a boy; she gave birth to a boy. He removed a collection of photographs from the drawer and carefully looked at each, photographs which he had taken, candid shots. 'Stephen had your eyes as well as your chin, the dimple was clear to see and became more pronounced as he grew up.' The last photograph was of him leaving through the school gates on his bicycle. He was waving to a friend. 'If you only knew how much I wanted to say hello. I knew you were mine.' He brought the photograph to his lips. 'I hope, wherever you are, you have now learned the truth.'

There was a tap on the door, and he quickly swept the photographs and the comic into the drawer as the door opened. It was Mark Hayes.

'I've just come through reception and Stacy has a keyboard problem. She asked if you'd take a look when you have a minute. I'm sure she makes up the problems just so you'll pop down.' He smiled, raised an eyebrow but then paused. 'Are you alright? You look as though you've seen a ghost.'

'Thanks, I'm, fine. I'll pop down and take a look shortly. Might be my lucky day.'

'Indeed, but don't call me shortly!' Mark winked and closed the door.

Opening the hastily closed drawer, he put the photographs back in chronological order, returned the news cuttings to the comic and closed it.

Staring at the window he knew that he had only one last task to rid himself of the hatred he had carried for so long. The excitement reaffirming his belief was no longer there. He checked the date. 'Tomorrow night and then, no more.'

* * *

The Pier Head was busy for a late afternoon. It posed as a magnet for tourists. Many came to pay homage to the four young men who had brought joy to millions with their music. But the draw was also the magic of the city's past, its history and beauty. In Alan's short life, he had begun to feel pride in his home city, it had moved on from when his grandad was a boy, and from what he could see, it was for the better. Somehow it seemed vibrant.

A number of metal barriers had been erected as workers were finalising the exhibits for the River of Light Festival. He studied a pamphlet he had collected from tourist information as he checked each location. Set in one of the renovated docks were large, fluorescent, rainbow-coloured floating spheres of different sizes. Along the dockside were what looked to be giant buttons. To Alan it was a huge bubble bath.

Tomorrow night, this area would be teeming with old and young alike. He would follow the instructions he had received and at the end of the walk he would be paid; as far as he was concerned, it would be the final closure. He could just disappear and start afresh.

* * *

Matthew Smith's mother was at the front window when the police car pulled up. She immediately answered the door.

'He can't have done owt as he's been in A&E all morning.'

She noticed him being helped out from the back of the police car by one of the officers. Although his limp was pronounced, he slipped past his mum without saying a word and went straight upstairs.

'And you can get your backside down here now. What the fuck's going on?' Her shrill scream made the officer take a step backwards. Matthew, otherwise known as Smigga, did not need asking twice. Her hand clipped the back of his head as he moved to the living room.

'You'd best come in.' She moved inside leaving the door open and the officers followed.

'Are you aware your Matthew is on post-charge bail? He was one of six people responsible for shoplifting, burglary and aggravated burglary. You might also have seen there have been two murders in the city recently, and there's a link to the six people, a connection to Matthew.'

'You saying he's killed people?' His mother frowned turning her attention to her son.

'Linked, which could make the offence extremely serious.'

'What link?'

Matthew stood in front of the settee and answered before he sat down.

'We wore red hoods, and the dead people were found wearing the same thing. I didn't kill anyone, mum. I told them that at the station. I knew nothing until one of the lads told me about it.'

'Who's got to you Matthew? You didn't limp, you didn't have any broken bones or stiches when you left the station.' One of the officers crouched in front of him. 'The others are out on bail, too. Will the same happen to them?'

His mother did not wait for an answer. Looking at the officer she answered for him. 'He told me he fell off Alan Green's motorbike.' As she spoke, she turned to observe Matthew and immediately could sense his panic. 'You bloody well didn't fall off his bike, did you?' Moving towards him, she raised her hand. 'What the bloody hell happened? Tell me now or I'll be sending you back needing more bloody medical attention.' She moved even closer, and he instinctively curled up in the seat.

'Sorry, no, sorry! He thought I'd grassed on him. He'd heard I had.'

'And that's the result?' Queried the officer, as his colleague went outside and called control seeking Alan Green's details. 'He only heard hearsay, and he did that to you? What will he do to you if he knows you've grassed on him? You play with some dangerous people, Matthew. If we arrest him, he'll definitely think you did tell and then what? What exactly do you know?'

Colin Drake received the call from Control.

'Colin, another of the Red Hoods has come to light. His name's Alan Green. Let's just say he has an interesting history. Matthew Smith has had a severe beating at the hands of Green. Officers attending managed to get a confession. Green thought he'd grassed. Mother's co-operating otherwise we'd have got nothing from him.'

'Wise mother. What about Green?'

'Officers are attending. They'll be at Green's soon enough. According to Matthew Smith, Green was responsible for collecting the instructions and dealing with the person to whom they refer as The Controller. Smith has been assured that the information he has offered will be treated in confidence. The lad's already suffered a severe beating along with a broken collar bone. It was Green with an iron bar.'

'In the library,' he muttered. 'Bloody hell it's like bloody Cluedo! I wonder what else Smith knows? Funny thing being a copper, as one door slams shut in your face another one opens. You've made my bloody day. Please keep me informed and I'll look forward to welcoming Mr Green.'

* * *

PC Gill Inman pushed the empty beer can away from the gate as she checked the address and approached the front door.

'Whatever you want him for he's not here.' Mrs Green stood in the doorway, her arms crossed beneath her ample bosom, her dressing gown wrapped around her as she stared at the officer. 'What's he supposed to have done now?'

'May we come in?' The officer requested as her finger switched on her bodycam. 'For your information I'm recording this interview. Are you alone in the house?'

'I have a friend here, a gentleman friend, but I don't see what business that is of yours.'

'When was Alan last here, Mrs Green?'

'This morning. We had tea, and he said he was going off for a few days. He does that every now and again, says he needs space, probably to get away from you lot. A change of people and scenery, and, if you look round here, you can hardly blame him. I'd be off if I could win the bloody lottery or meet a rich bloke.

My Alan has always been picked on ever since he was a nipper. First it was the bloody teachers, then you lot, the coppers. Wouldn't leave the poor lad alone. He's a good boy. Loves his mum.'

'He's a man, and he's given someone a severe beating. We could look round and go, or we could get a search warrant and really look into every nook and cranny, but the choice is yours.'

'Step into the lounge. My friend can leave, and then you can take a look round, but you'll not find him here. You'll have to excuse the mess. I've had a busy week.'

CHAPTER 32

Green sat on the capstan, his rucksack by his feet. Removing the instructions, he read the note again. It seemed so simple, maybe too simple:

At 7.30, walk from the capstan to the captain. You must be wearing a red hood at all times. On arrival, slip the hood over the captain's outstretched hand. Return to the capstan and your reward will be waiting. Don't bother to search before you set off, it will not be there until your return. However, I shall be watching you every inch of the way.

It made absolutely no sense, but for four grand, he'd walk bare arsed to Bootle and back. Out of curiosity, he checked every orifice around the top of the capstan. He was rewarded with only rubbish.

Collecting his bag, he walked the route he would take the following evening. Now it was still light, but at the time he had been told to walk, it would be dusk, and the number of people attracted to the opening of the festival would be far greater.

Checking the time on his phone, he was dismayed to find the walk had taken over twenty-five minutes to complete. Wearing a red hood, he would stand out like a sore thumb. The route he had chosen was the one he believed would have the fewest number of people but of that he could not be certain.

His stomach rumbled. He needed to eat and return to his sanctuary.

* * *

Skeeter stood in the Incident Room. The news regarding Smith and Green had brought hope in discovering more and possibly identifying the link between The Controller and the gang. Even though it was getting late, Drake had brought Rathbone back for interview. He was considered the weakest link and the one more likely to snap under pressure. Skeeter needed to watch the interview and settled before the monitor that was linked to the interview room. It was clear from the start that Rathbone was more nervous than she had expected. He began his foot-tapping as he waited with the custody officer and the duty solicitor.

Drake said nothing as he entered, just proffered a courteous nod to the solicitor before placing a file on the table.

'Mr Rathbone. Tell me what you know about Alan.' He clasped his hands and sat back.

John Rathbone flushed and started to chew his lip as he turned to his solicitor, who did not respond but looked at his own notes.

'He, he was in the gang. He was our leader, a boss in a way.'

'I know that, John. What else?'

He looked sideways again, and on this occasion, the solicitor returned his glance. 'Tell the officer what you know. All of it. Now is the right time.'

'What if Greenie finds out I've said something?'

There was silence in the room, and his foot bounced even faster.

'He got the instructions. He told us what to do. He was the boss as I said.'

'What do you know about this controller chap?'

He shook his head. 'Nothing. Nobody saw him, but Smigga believed he was at the robberies, watching. I didn't see him. It all happened so quick. He told us what to do. He made us do the hoods. I've told you I sewed them following his instructions. They all had to be different.'

'Did he know which ones you each wore?'

John shook his head. 'Only Greenie knew. He could tell one from the other.'

'So, you never met him? Greenie didn't meet him, but he spoke with him?'

'Only on the phone. I don't know how it started. We had phones. We nicked them so we weren't short. Throwaways, he called them. Green got a call, but it lasted two rings and then stopped. That was the signal. The next time it rang it would be him, The Controller.'

'Where did you meet, John? To discuss what you had to do, to share the money.'

'The dragon's e ...' He shook his head.

Drake said nothing but looked directly at John. 'Smigga, is like you, John. He's on bail. Unfortunately, your friend has spent the morning at the hospital. Do you know why?'

Rathbone frowned and shook his head.

'He met up with your other friend, Alan Green. According to his mum, Greenie took an iron bar to him. The doctor said he could have been killed. Bad gash to his head. It's all stitched up. Broken collar bone and severe damage to his knee. Now why would a friend do that to a friend?'

Skeeter looked at Rathbone's face on the screen. Drake had certainly brought a degree of reality to the interview.

'You do know, after this chat, you will be walking out of the station or possibly be dropped off at your house in a marked police car. Unfortunately, John, as I said, we have no idea where Green is at this moment in time. Let me ask again. Where did you all meet up? Could he be there? Is it a place in which he could hide? What information did he think Smith might have told us?'

'I don't know. I never went to the meetings. I received my money when we just met up with those who drove. The riders met. Smigga, Greenie and Sparra but we didn't.'

'So, what's "the dragon?" That's what you said.'

'Honest, I heard them talk about a dragon's eye, but they didn't say anything else.'

Drake checked his watch. 'Interview stopped at 17.56. You're free to leave. We'll be calling you back in if we find out more information. If you bump into Smith, you might ask him what the hell is going on. If you see Alan Green, please tell him we're looking for him.' He looked at the duty solicitor. 'Take as much time as you need. If your client knows what's in his best interests, he might just talk to you. Thanks. Take care, John.' Drake left the room. Skeeter was waiting in the corridor.

'Frightened shitless, if you want my professional opinion, Colin. He realises the precarious position he's in. I think he'll squeal.'

* * *

Skeeter was preparing to leave. That evening she had planned to work with the kids at the wrestling club. She would train first and then let the pressures of work fade by helping the nippers.

'I hoped I'd catch you.' Michael was carrying a coffee as he approached her desk.

'You look as though you've not slept for a week,' Skeeter announced as she slipped on her coat.

'Not funny, Wicca. I'll get up to speed with the case during my shift, but I managed to read your notes of the interview with Rob Duncan. There's a man who walks the thin line of the living. Two deaths with two relationships, Kate and the child, Stephen. He believed the father of the child was a doctor. Seems strange that he knew very little, but he learned that. There's a clue worth chasing.' He sipped his coffee and looked for her approval.

'Here's another to play havoc with the circadian rhythm. The dragon's eye. It was just mentioned in an interview with John Rathbone, and I can assure you that he wasn't referring to me as I was out of the room! Possibly a meeting place. I'll just park that there and wish you a good evening. If you do discover anything, don't call me until at least seven tomorrow morning. Must fly!'

Michael started to look around.

'What have you lost?'

'Looking for your broomstick.'

Skeeter raised her middle finger and grinned.

Even as Skeeter threw the heavy leather wrestling dummy over her shoulder, she found her mind drifting to the interviews that afternoon. Normally, the feel of the worn, rough leather and the smell of sweat inspired her to train hard and forget the troubles of the day, but, for some reason, her enthusiasm had deserted her. It was only the sound of the kids, the Tumble Tots, arriving, their eager screams and chatter echoing around her, that allowed work to be forgotten if only for an hour or so.

Alan Green pulled the sleeping bag tightly to his chin. The idea of spending a few nights beneath the eye had seemed quite adventurous in the light of day, but now, in the dark, he was not too sure. For the first time, for as long as he could remember, he felt alone. In the darkness, the severity of his actions became clear. How could he ever believe his past would not catch up with him? The ground was as unforgiving as his new-found conscience, and they contrived to deny him sleep. Even his most basic needs proved an annoyance. After careful contemplation, he had decided to use the left passageway as his toilet. Having no running water, no way of washing his hands brought a swift realisation that the home, his home, the one he considered to be nothing more than a shit house, was better than this. The cavernous space had never seemed to be damp nor cold in the short time they had spent there but as the night wore on, its whole ambience changed. The cold seemed to conspire with the rough ground and nag him awake. He made up his mind that two nights spent there would be one too many. Once he had the money, he could find somewhere warmer.

CHAPTER 33

Those in the briefing watched as April spoke to camera. The whole three minute video had been well co-ordinated and recorded earlier. The PCC press office had ensured it hit the local as well as the national news. The appeal was sincere and strong with the initial focus on the revelation of a red hood. She included the links to the comic series. April provided details of the person they were wanting for questioning and included the still shot of the man's reflection captured in the pub. She emphasised the words 'professional', 'doctor' and 'local man' to give a clear impression. Details of those killed were also sensitively shared. At the end of the statement, a photograph of Alan Green filled the screen. 'We believe this man may have vital information about this case. If you know of his whereabouts or you see him, we advise that he is not approached but for you to contact Merseyside Police on the numbers on screen, through our social media pages or Crimestoppers. Anonymity will be guaranteed.'

The necessary staffing was also ready to man the phones. Skeeter left with Drake. He wanted one last shot at Micky Webster.

'He's hiding something, but it's getting him to talk.'

Skeeter's mobile rang. 'Michael?'

'It's later than you said, but I've been chasing a few further clues. I saw the appeal. It was excellent. Hope you've prepared for the cranks and the nutters.'

'Love your professional enthusiasm, Michael.'

'It's being so cheerful that keeps me going, Wicca. Anyway, that's not what I wanted you for. I've been chatting to a guy called Joseph Lee. He's an amateur explorer of ruins and underground works. I was chasing the dragon's eye you mentioned, and I discovered a video on YouTube. It's located in a local stone mine. He explored it about eighteen months ago and since then, owing to its being on private land, the area has been secured. Originally it was like an underground stone quarry, but then it was used to store ammunition during the Second World War, owing to the unusually dry conditions. He informed me the passageways are quite extensive. Within it, however, there's an orb in part of the ceiling that looks like a huge dragon's eye. I've sent you a link to the video he produced. He's also given me the location. As far as he's aware, the entrances have been sealed. He believes the official one is closed by steel doors, and the entrance he used has been barred and blocked. I've asked Phil Lipson to see if he can contact the owner of the land. It might also be worth sending a regular patrol over throughout the day just in case Green is staying there. That's me done.'

After she had finished the call, Colin had long gone. She made her way to the Interview Room. They were already present when she arrived. Michael Webster watched her enter and take a seat.

'Bloody hell, it's a witch. Bringing the frightening ones with you this time?'

His solicitor said nothing. He had heard much worse.

'Micky, a little bird has told us that you did a bad, bad thing.

What might that bad thing be?' Drake did not look up but flicked through the papers within the file.

'You told me I'd stabbed someone, but then you said something about a DNA match. What happened there, officer? I've done nothing. Ask him.' He pointed to the solicitor who shook his head.

'Cast your mind back. Paradise Street and Hanover Street. A motorcycle, electric, silent. Bringing back any memories?'

'I don't shop at John Lewis, so, no.'

'There was a handbag snatch. A young woman. You, I'm informed, grabbed the bag. Alan Green was your pilot on that day. The sad part of this was the young woman was tougher than many of your victims, and she kept a tight hold of her bag. Do you want to tell me the rest?'

'What the fuck are you talking about? I haven't a clue. Ask her, she might have a crystal ball.'

'Let me remind you, you've been cautioned, and you've also been charged with robbery, use of an illegal motor vehicle and GBH. What else do we not know?' Skeeter chipped in.

'Fuck, it speaks.'

'Do excuse him, and don't let him anger you, DS Warlock. As what you're about to say might even things out.' Drake slipped a piece of paper in front of her. There was a silence as she read it before continuing.

'Thick-skinned, Mr Webster. We witches tend to be.' She stared at Webster and back at the note before she read what was written down. 'Michael Webster,' she paused. 'I am arresting you for the murder of Kate Nolan.' She gave the date and the time. 'You were the pillion rider on a motorcycle driven by Alan Green.'

Webster observed Skeeter before turning to his solicitor. Skeeter looked at Drake and raised an eyebrow.

'Fucking Smigga, the lying two-faced gobshite. It was a fucking accident.'

On leaving, Skeeter took Drake's arm. 'Thanks for the info. Where did that come from?'

'We received a call from Matthew Smith's mother this morning when you were chatting to Michael. He'd had a dreadful night, "frightened shitless" if I can use her term. Apparently, he went to her in the night and told her that Webster had confessed to him when drunk, that he and Green had killed a woman. Apparently, at the time, they were unaware she'd died. It was only later, when they saw the news, they realised what had happened. Smigga had revealed to Green what Webster had told him, and that resulted in the beating. Thought you might like to deal the crucial blow.'

Skeeter leaned against the wall as a puzzled look spread across her face. 'Too bloody right. A cold case no longer, thanks for that. I owe you. Now I need to see Phil Lipson. He might just know where we can find Green. Can you get someone to Green's house? If you can, I want her phone checking, she might have her son's number. If she does have, he's not as bright as I thought.'

CHAPTER 34

Skeeter, Phil and two other officers pulled up along the narrow lane looking for the address. They approached the small, brick-built bungalow set well off the road. Skeeter thought the tree-topped hill standing immediately behind the house looked man-made. To the left of the entrance to the driveway was a long wooden garage that had seen better times, as had much of the surrounding garden to the house. Walking up the unmade drive, Skeeter noticed a person come out of a greenhouse as another approached from the front door of the house. She paused. Both men looked identical. She took a second glance.

'Mr Finch?' she asked, turning to the man who was closer.

They answered in unison and chuckled. 'It happens all the time. Identical twins, you see. Confuses a lot of folk when we first meet.'

Both men were in their seventies and looked in rude health. Skeeter smiled as she noticed that even their overalls were a match.

'DS Warlock, and this is DC Lipson. Thanks for agreeing to

see us.' The two uniformed officers remained further down the drive.

'I'm Thomas, and this is Jeremy.' He paused and looked at his brother before they moved towards Skeeter. He could see her puzzled look. 'We know, Tom and Jerry, but we've learned to live with it. Let's just say it was an innocent mistake on our parents' behalf. That's why ...' Thomas was interrupted.

'We never like to shorten our names,' Jeremy concluded.

'Have you come about the quarry? It's been a right pain since the post on the internet appeared, but we have it secured again. We can never tell how safe the roof is. Once we thought of opening it up to the public, but the legal side was daunting, so it stays locked or until the government wants to store ammunition there again. That could be sooner than we realise.'

'Lots of local kids used to come and mess about, but they did no real damage. Then we found it was being used for sex, drugs and rocks without the roll.' They both laughed together, it was obviously a favourite joke. Skeeter could hardly keep up as each man ended the other's sentences.

Alan Green had seen the cars pass along the narrow lane, and he remained within the sparse wooded area. His heart missed a beat on seeing one was marked 'Police'. He had a good vantage point, and he took a minute to calm down. He had secured the narrow entrance he used by placing the stones precisely then, taking a photograph with his phone. He could check and ensure they had not been moved should he return.

Keeping to the fields, he made his way to the main road. He would soon be in town and relatively safe. He would not be back, and if an alternative could not be found, it would have to be a last resort.

* * *

The small, steel door set within two larger hangar-type doors protested as it opened. Skeeter felt a breath of air pass her.

'That's the dragon's breath. It's usually warm, especially in summer when the sun heats the domed land above,' Thomas said with a wink, as Jeremy brought two large torches and handed one to his brother. 'Black as pitch once you're away from this door. It can seem quite a warren if you've not been in here before. Just watch where you put your feet.' Thomas moved in first.

'How far is the dragon's eye?' Skeeter asked. She had seen the video and was keen to see the actual roof section.

'A few minutes, five at the most. These concrete pillars hold the roof but there are some made from thousands of pieces of stone. Our father revealed it was full of ammunition boxes at one time, brought from factories in Kirkby. The doors at the entrance are bomb proof.'

The torch light bounced across the passageway as they made their way further down.

'There's the dragon's eye, but we are near the top. To get a better view we need to descend.'

The sleeping bag was the first thing Skeeter saw. She pointed to it. 'That looks new.' She took the torch and searched the rest of the cavern. The bike wheel was the next thing, then further away, the frame. The others quickly took up the search. Jeremy came back holding one of the red hoods.

'There's more stuff over there.'

'A veritable Aladdin's cave,' Lipson observed as he held open the hood.

'And there's your dragon's eye.' Thomas held the torch to the ceiling. 'You can see the staining that gives it the appearance of an eye. It's as close to a circle as you can get. It's formed by the delamination of the roof's rock layers. Quite magical.'

Skeeter stared at it, her mouth agape. 'That's amazing. What a natural wonder!'

Thomas grinned. 'No matter how many times we come down here it still has the power to amaze.'

CHAPTER 35

Much of what had been discovered in the cavern had been removed by a team of crime scene forensic officers, and Skeeter was in little doubt they had discovered where Green had spent the night since leaving home. CCTV footage from the local Go Outdoors in the city centre had revealed that Green had purchased a few items. The video was added to the facial recognition data and would be actively tracking as soon as possible.

'I've asked the Finch twins to keep an eye on the cave, and we've added a light sensor inside the other known entry points. Should they be triggered we can have a dog patrol there within fifteen minutes.'

April saw Lucy running towards her glass office. *Never seen her run before!* she thought.

Lucy entered. 'Control has picked up a call generated by your appeal. It's from a Mr Mark Hayes. He wouldn't give any details over the phone but hoped someone could call and see him after 4pm. The person taking the call has noted that there was uncertainty in his voice as if he wasn't sure he was doing the right thing. He didn't want to waste our valuable time.'

'That makes a change. I like him already,' Skeeter announced.

'He has work commitments until then. He left an address and a phone number.'

'What do we know about him?' April took the note and started to check the address on Google Earth.

'Nothing as far as I'm aware. It's just come in.'

'Lives on the Wirral, Little Sutton.' She glanced at the clock on the screen. 'You and Tony.' She looked at Skeeter. 'Kasum and Phil will be out for the start of the River of Light Festival. There are twelve light installations within a three kilometre walk taking in the key locations. The theme this year is Play. I just don't want the bikes roaming freely.'

'And the VOI rentals, the e-bikes and scooters?'

'I'm assured that owing to the installed GPS software, certain areas are out of bounds. Remember also, renters have to take a selfie before hiring the bikes, so there's a comprehensive log of users. The fear is about those in private hands. There will be CCTV, facial recognition and fast response teams, the same as for concerts and football matches. There's nothing new in this.'

Skeeter collected Tony who was checking his teeth using the camera on his phone.

'Seven years bad luck if you break a mirror, not so sure for the screen on a camera. Give us a clue.'

Tony turned and grinned. 'My first dental visit for years.'

She struggled to inspect his teeth and was stunned considering the state they had been in. 'I'm impressed.'

He spread his lips as wide as possible.

'Dazzling. Well done. All you need to do is clean them twice a day. Grab your coat.'

'Bloody hell, I hope they'll have that effect on all the girls!'

* * *

Alan avoided any corporate food outlets and found a small café off the dock road. He was surprised at its cleanliness. He ordered an all-day breakfast, it might be his only meal. The TV was on, but the only other person was reading the racing page of his newspaper. He had not lifted his head up since his arrival.

'Food won't be a minute love. Always like to make sure the sausages are well done don't I, Don?'

The lone figure turned to her and smiled. 'That's a fact, Betty. You cook a good sausage.'

'Not working today, love?' The lady wiped the counter top clean.

Alan shook his head. 'Not today. Is it alright if I charge my phone?' He pointed to the socket. 'Forgot last night, and I'll be lost without it.'

'Course you can. You young ones and your phones. What would you do without them?' True to her word she brought out his order. 'Added an extra sausage, look as though you need feeding up.' She grinned as she wiped her hands on her apron. 'Sauces and eating irons are over there. I'll get your bread and butter and your tea. Enjoy.'

Alan had never before eaten so slowly. He needed to kill time. He wanted to avoid the Pier Head until such time as he needed to be there. The main shopping centre was to be avoided. He ordered a coffee for his flask.

As he paid, the lady pushed a foil pack over to him. 'Made you a couple of bacon butties, on the house, like. You seem a bit down in the dumps. Whatever's bothering you, love, I hope you get it sorted soon.'

Alan pulled up his hood and walked away with his head down. He was just grateful it was not raining.

* * *

Once over the Mersey Gateway Bridge, Tony turned towards Chester on the M56. The estimated time for the journey was twenty-eight minutes. The traffic was slower than anticipated, but they had time in hand. Skeeter checked the address. As they turned onto Heath Way they slowed, as the satnav announced the location was on their left.

'A tenner says he's a bloody time waster.' Tony announced as he climbed from the car.

Mark Hayes was expecting them, and the front door opened as they approached.

'Mr Hayes?'

'Thanks for taking the time to come out. I do hope I've not brought you on a wild goose chase but since seeing the appeal I …'

Skeeter held up her hand. 'DS Warlock and this is DC Price. May we?'

'Yes, goodness. You can see how anxious I am. Do. To the right and take a seat. May I get you a tea or coffee?'

Skeeter declined, much to Tony's annoyance.

'I work at Stanlow. I'm a chemist but I predominantly deal with the quality management of …' He stopped. 'That's really immaterial. It was the hood, and the description of the person for whom you are searching that made me contact you. I work with a lovely chap. He had a breakdown, mental issues. I think it was either May or June last year he had the trouble. He lives in Crosby, but he loves New Brighton. His problem started after he tried to save a young girl who'd been swept into the sea from some steps on which she was playing. Quite the hero act; he could have been killed! Although he managed to get the girl to the steps and onto the promenade, unfortunately, she died. It was in the local paper, and I believe briefly mentioned nationally. "Super Hero Fails to Save Drowning Girl" … One thing stuck in my mind. I went to his office not long afterwards, a couple of days at most, and found him in tears. It wasn't only because she had died, but during his attempt to save her, people just videoed the event rather than assisting. I think it pushed him over the edge. Do either of you have children?'

They answered in the negative.

'I have a daughter, so I thought about her and tried to visualise her drowning and people standing by doing nothing. I realised it would take me over the edge, too.'

Tony turned to Skeeter and then back to Hayes. They could sense his anger.

'He seemed to cope well at first, but then went to pieces, as I said, he had a mental breakdown. He was awarded compassionate leave, of course, and then, when he was medically deemed to be recovering, he was brought back into work on a phased induction programme. He's only just back to full time, which tells you how badly he was affected, and I must say, even now, he's not like his old self. He's lost his sense of humour, but he does a good job. PTSD was diagnosed, and you'll know from your profession how life changing that can be.'

'Do you have a name?' Skeeter probed.

'Goodness me, yes. Do I have your assurance that this will be handled in the strictest confidence?'

'Of course. You also mentioned the hoods.'

'Yes, sorry. His name is Dr Owen Baron. He's an engineer specialising in computer science, he's not medical. A few days ago, I called into his office, and on his desk was a comic. He was very defensive when I entered, and he tried to cover it up. I have to say we had a bit of a lad's joke about that. Anyway, it turned out to be about a character called Red Hood. He informed me it was linked to Batman and Robin. He mentioned something about Stephen liking them, too, but I don't know who that is.'

It was Skeeter's turn to look at Tony.

'I thought nothing of it until this morning. I came into work and checked with personnel the days Owen was in work against the reports of the two deaths. He was off all or part of those days. Something else, he's obsessed with the knot on his tie. He's forever adjusting it.'

'Do you have his address?'

Hayes stood. 'It's in Crosby. Just a second.' He collected his phone. He read the details out and Tony made a note.

'Strictest confidence and I'm sure you'll handle it with the utmost discretion after all, as I said, I may have set you on the wrong course.'

'Thank you very much. You've been most helpful.' Tony shook his hand.

'Before you go, the one thing that convinced me to contact you was the image in the mirror. That, in my eyes, was Owen. Even though it was quite blurred, I knew straight away.'

'Was he in work today?'

'Mostly, yes, but he left early, about two. He normally would work until four. When I saw him, he looked as though he'd seen a ghost. Maybe it was a bad day.'

In the car, Skeeter held her hand flat towards Tony. 'That's a tenner, buddy. I think we've found our man. However, I have a nag. Just what did Rob Duncan know really?'

'Never presume, it might not be the same Stephen.'

On the way to Crosby, Skeeter called in the details they had received. There was still no sighting of Green.

CHAPTER 36

There was nobody in at Owen Baron's home, and the neighbour had not seen him all day. A twenty-four-hour watch was placed on the house.

Skeeter and Tony stood in Dr Baron's office in front of an imposing desk. The negotiations had taken longer than either had anticipated. Two security officers belonging to the firm monitored their actions as Skeeter picked up the framed photograph from the desk. She turned it to Tony who shrugged his shoulders. She photographed it. Trying the long top drawer, she found it locked.

'Do you have a key?'

From a large bunch of keys attached to a chain, the security officer came round the desk. He inspected the lock and selected two keys. The first was unsuccessful but the second one turned freely in the lock. Skeeter slipped on a pair of nitrile gloves before sliding it open. Tony moved next to her. The three numbered phones were to the side of the comic. The red hood character stared back. Tony videoed the proceeding. Leaving the comic in the drawer, she opened it showing the two news cuttings.

Holding up the news cuttings, she paused before glancing out of the large window and across to the island and the vast expanse of water. The clouds and the river seemed to merge perfectly, but then she caught her reflection, it was vague and yet real. She immediately felt as though she were in the river itself, immersed within the watery scene.

'The drowning. Bloody hell, Stephen's drowning. Bloody hell. They both drowned, Stephen and the girl Mark Hayes told us about.' She turned back to the desk picking up the photographs before laying them in order on the desk; all the while Tony videoed her actions. She pointed to the picture of the lad on the bike between the gates. 'Where have you seen the likes of that before?'

'Michael's Batman image at the gates. They are different and yet ...'

Within the hour they had forwarded the video to April and were approaching Speke.

* * *

Dr Owen Baron sat on the concrete steps with his back to the buildings that made up the Three Graces. A light mist clung immobile to the river's surface even though the tidal flow clearly moved the water beneath; it was heading out to the mouth of the estuary. The occasional lights on the far bank were now visible along its length, their reflections pointing wavily across towards him as if floating on the grey, hazy bed. The noise in the background, the people eager to experience the start of the River of Light Festival, grew and echoed along George's Parade.

He withdrew the silver frame from his pocket. Stephen stared back, his arm waving. It was a child he knew so well but did not know at all. He brought it to his lips and kissed the glass as he had done so many times before. Removing the photograph, he walked to the wooden, capped safety rail that ran the length of the river's edge and tossed the frame into the water. It seemed to float momentarily before sinking and disappearing.

The Liver Building clock showed the time was 7.12. One of the exhibitions was well on the way as people walked along piano keys which changed the colours of the lights whilst creating different sounds. The crowd's attention was on this spectacle and not on the river's edge. He watched for a moment whilst standing in front of the statue before him. Here, too, was a man who had lost a son, lost him to a watery grave. Why had he, the captain, had the strength to remain so brave, so focused? He reflected on the many times Stephen's memory had crushed him, leaving him paralysed, fragile and angry. He slipped and trapped the photograph beneath the captain's bronze boot. He now had one more battle, one more act of cleansing to complete. This was not random. He had planned it so precisely. He looked up at the bronze face of the captain and felt his hand move to his head, as if in salute. The next death, Green's death, might just set him free, a freedom for which he longed. Within moments, he set off towards the Museum of Liverpool and the bridge that crosses the dock gates leading to the Albert Dock. Whichever route Alan Green took, he would have to cross at this point to arrive at the captain. It was now all about the wait. The darkness had quickly fallen, and the pathways were lit.

At the same time, Alan was sitting on the capstan in the growing dark. There were few people in the area as he was away from any of the light exhibitions. The red hood was in his hands. His heart fluttered. He could not remember the last time he had felt so nervous, so apprehensive. His phone rang. He waited. After the second ring, it stopped.

'Come on! Let's get this done.'

When it rang again, he answered immediately. 'Greenie, I see you're there,' Owen guessed. 'You'll be starting your walk soon. Do remember your instructions.'

The voice was different. There was not a hint of a Scouse accent. Alan's apprehension grew. 'Fuck you, whoever you are.'

Slipping on the hood, he stood, face down, before pulling up his jacket hood to conceal as much as possible of the vivid red. He started his challenge. 'Walk fast, walk fast and keep your head down,' he said as he began to walk. Stuffing his hands into his pockets, he ignored anyone passing by. More people began to appear the closer he got to the dock, but he remained on the river side, only breaking away from the comparative safety as he approached the narrow swing bridge that crossed the lock gates. It had been divided by metal barriers to allow pedestrians to cross in one-way flows. Fluorescent-jacketed security officers ensured the now growing crowds followed the signs. Alan paused but then moved in the crowd keeping his head down.

At the other side, and looking across towards the opposite flow of people, was Owen Baron. He spotted Green immediately. His efforts at concealment made him even more noticeable. Baron tapped a security officer on the shoulder and pointed in Green's direction. The security officer instinctively jumped the barrier causing the noise from the crowd to rise. Alan heard this and looked up. The red hood stared directly towards Baron and the fast-moving fluorescent jacket. Alan could not go backwards, and the compact flow of pedestrians before him had slowed to almost a standstill. Like a trapped animal, desperate to escape, he looked quickly around. If he could jump from the bridge to the ledge at the side of the lock towards the round building to his left, he could then mix with the growing crowd that seemed to be moving freely.

He mounted the flat, metal edge of the bridge amidst the bustle and shouts. The salty dew on the lip made his foot slip, and he fell sideways. His right hand grabbed the rail top as he dangled over the dark, watery mouth of the dock entrance. His body hovered ten feet above the unforgiving eddies and curling tidal water. The first security officer grabbed Green's wrist with both hands – the red hood staring up at him, menacing and unfathomable. One of his hands slipped, but he managed to grab Green's arm again. With his free hand, Alan caught hold of a rail that controlled his swinging body.

Baron watched as the drama unfolded. Leaning over the edge, he surveyed the void as the liquid swirled and bubbled below. It was not what he had planned, but to his excitement and pleasure it was turning out to be the very scene depicted in the comic. In his confused and disturbed mind, the black cape he knew from the story was now fluorescent yellow – they were enacting the scene from the comic perfectly. The cameras were out, and recordings and photographs were being taken. A second security officer pushed through the crowd and grabbed Green's other hand; together they dragged him back over the bridge rail. Within his peripheral vision, Owen Baron noticed the police officers running towards the bridge. Alan Green was quickly lost amongst four security officers. Turning to head back towards the captain, he saw more police appearing from either side of Mann Island. Baron moved quickly to his right, focusing on the ship's large propeller, a monument to Liverpool's past. To his surprise, the police, too, changed direction, and he quickly realised that he had become their target. He did not see the person whose arm tucked beneath his, but he felt a leg wrap behind his knee, and before he knew it, he was looking at the sky. His back hit the cobbles hard and his breath was driven out uncontrollably. Skeeter swiftly rolled him onto his stomach and brought his right arm up his back. She grinned at Tony.

CHAPTER 37

Two days later

'Bloody hell, April, she was like lightning. He was arse over tit before he could say Bob's your uncle.' Tony had told everyone more than once what he had witnessed. 'He'd been staring at a camera for ten minutes, our hidden eye. Facial recognition told us exactly where he was and Green came as a bonus.'

Skeeter said nothing. 'According to Green, he had to get to the statue of Captain Walker whilst wearing the red hood. He doesn't know why, other than for the cash that was promised. According to Smith, he was always up for a dare. Anyway, an officer found that photograph under the boot on the statue and yet, there was no cash when the capstan was checked!'

Kasum stared at the image on the large screen. 'During his interview, he had said how Penny had goaded him, she would never admit that the child she was carrying was his. I believe, from what Owen Baron said, she was free with her favours. That's why he left, although she convinced everyone he'd deserted her on hearing of the pregnancy. According to his strong protestations, nothing could be further from the truth. He was sure the child, Stephen, was his. He monitored the boy's progress. The candid, photographic evidence of this was in his desk. They tracked his growing up.'

'So why the comic, the hoods?' Tony asked. 'This picture and the film?'

'As far as the professional psychiatric assessment is concerned, it stemmed from his attempt to save the child in New Brighton. He sought vengeance. Those videoing the drama and the news cutting of the upturned car took him to the edge, and he vowed he'd get his revenge, twisted as it appears to us. He thought the killings would cleanse his mind and free him from the guilt he felt over giving up on his son. Stephen had drowned, and so, too, the girl. It affected him profoundly. Using the bikes was inspired by the photographs of his son and the image taken from the film. Correct, Tony. He could find his victims, his medicine to heal his disturbed mind. However, as you're now aware, from the clues he has provided, we can be assured we'll never be able to locate Penny. He'll say no more, but I'm sure you can draw your own conclusions.'

Skeeter looked at Tony. 'An intelligent man with a strong yearning for vengeance is a formidable foe, Tony. Thank goodness I work with someone who's as safe as bloody houses.' She grinned at him then winked at Kasum.

THE PIER HEAD

At the end of each book, I try to highlight one area featured in the novel.

The Pier Head features throughout this story and it is a location I have known since I was young. My Uncle Alan lived in Upton on the Wirral and worked in the city of Liverpool. I have memories of travelling with him on the Mersey Ferry in the sixties and landing at the Pier Head in front of the wonderful buildings known as the Three Graces: the Royal Liver Building, the Cunard Building and the Port of Liverpool Building make a wonderful and majestic backdrop and skyline. How different it was then!

The jewel, in my eyes, has always been the Liver Building, a huge wedding cake of a building that is now open to visitors. I would highly recommend the tour if you have an hour to spare and a head for heights. It will bring you face to face with the magical Liver Birds. I love this historical description taken from *Visit Liverpool*.

The tale of the two Liver Birds relates to the city's maritime heritage. The Liver Bird that looks over the Mersey River is said to represent the wives who stay at home and look out to their sailor husbands away at sea. The Liver Bird that looks over the city represents these sailors out at sea, looking back over to the city and their family.

Many changes have been made to the area making it very people friendly. The routing of the canal you will know about if you have read *Edge of the Land*. The development of the large open spaces is now home to concerts and festivals as well as the inclusion of the many memorials and statues. The most visited and photographed is the statue to the four young Liverpudlians, The Beatles, but there are many others. I focused on one in this book that I love to visit, that of Captain Frederic 'Johnnie' Walker. Sadly, it is often ignored by many who promenade along the water side, and yet he was a true hero in every sense of the word, a man who put his country first. If you do spend some time in Liverpool, then do enjoy a quiet moment in his company.

The Pier Head continues to be developed, and the many exciting changes not only reflect the fashions of the day but pay homage to the past. The Pier Head is the perfect place to stop the clock, sit and enjoy the wonderful city spread before you or just watch the waters of the Mersey flow with the tides as it has done for ever.

ABOUT THE AUTHOR

You could say that the writing was clearly on the wall for anyone born in a library that they might aspire to be an author but to get to that point, Malcolm Hollingdrake has travelled a circuitous route.

Malcolm worked in education for many years, even teaching for a period in Cairo before he started writing, a challenge he longed to tackle for more years than he cares to remember.

Malcolm has written a number of successful short stories and has more than ten books available (and more to come).

Born in Bradford and spending three years in Ripon, Malcolm has never lost his love for his home county, a passion that is reflected in the settings of fourteen Harrogate Crime Series novels.

Malcolm has enjoyed many hobbies including works by Northern artists; the art auctions offer a degree of excitement when both buying and certainly when selling. It's a hobby he has bestowed on DCI Cyril Bennett, of his characters in the Harrogate Crime Series.

ACKNOWLEDGMENTS

I did say that I had written my last book, so I must offer my apologies to Debbie, my ever-patient wife, who, somehow, knew another one was gestating. I could not write without her initial appraisal, her positive encouragement and the edit she so diligently completes. I love you. x

To Livia whose fault this book is for sending me a notebook entitled – *The Merseyside Series – continued*. It would have been a sin to leave it blank! Thank you for the kick I so desperately needed.

The beautiful city of Liverpool also seduced me into writing just one more book. I feel its very fabric becomes a real character, a familiar face moulded from the very waters of the Mersey and its ancient buildings and streets. The new dockside developments continue to grow, their gothic architectural style fed from the past and combined with the fresh creativity of today, in many ways unique. This brave rebirth ensures the area can enjoy a bright future, bringing many from around the world to marvel in the city's friendship and welcome.

Always, my first thanks must go to those Liverpudlians who patiently guide me and answer many of my questions. To the people responsible for the wonderful River of Light exhibitions, an imaginative, temporary, interactive festival that brought a throng of people to the waterfront and the surrounds, successfully bringing laughter, awe and wonder.

I must also thank those who guided me to secret locations

that should remain just that or become only fiction trapped within the pages of this book.

To Helen Gray, who has become a friend as well as my professional proof reader.

The same goes for Ian Cleverdon, who has followed my writing journey since before the pub burnt down! Thanks, Ian.

Thanks must go to the Hobeck Advanced Readers' Team for their guidance, support and encouragement. You are a vital cog in the machine.

All authors need their names whispered far and wide. This grapevine never happens by magic but by the determination of bloggers, readers' groups and internet groups who turn their hobby into a support system for authors and writers. Through administering social media groups, interviewing and talking about books to a broader audience, they bring books and authors into many homes. My sincere thanks.

My thanks to Donna Wilbor, Lynda Checkley and Donna Morfett for your dedicated support for my books. You have been with me from the beginning.

I must also thank people who have been so willing to become characters in this book. Kate Nolan and Tim Foxton, it was a pleasure to meet you. Nigel Chadburn, I hope you enjoyed your trip to Merseyside.

'So, what about the Red Hoods?' I hear you say. As it states in the story, wandering around second-hand book shops can lead to the formation of the most unusual ideas. That idea, mixed with childhood memories of racing waves on New Brighton promenade as a child without fear of the consequences, made the writing of some elements of this story so real.

To Hobeck Books, thank you for having confidence in my work and for the dedication you put in to make it the best it can be.

Finally, it is to you, dear readers, to whom I must say a

massive thank you for supporting my love of writing. Please keep passing on your kind words and reviewing the books you read. Those two steps can mean so much to the success of a book.

Best wishes,
Malcolm

What is this life if, full of care,
We have no time to stand and stare ...

William Henry Davies
'Leisure'

THE MERSEYSIDE CRIME SERIES

Catch as Catch Can

Syn

Edge of the Land

Available from Amazon and book retailers.

'Another must buy series.' ★★★★★

'I love words and this author is a master of painting a picture you can fall right into.' ★★★★★

'A stunning and flawless read.' ★★★★★

'OK I am hooked Mr Hollingdrake, I don't mind which book you write next but please write it soon!' ★★★★★

'Absolutely brilliant!' ★★★★★

HOBECK BOOKS – THE HOME OF GREAT STORIES

This book is the fourth in the Merseyside Crime Series.

If you've enjoyed this book, please visit Malcolm's website: **www.malcolmhollingdrakeauthor.co.uk** to read about his other writing, inspirations, writing life and for news about his forthcoming writing projects.

Hobeck Books offers a number of short stories and novellas, free for subscribers in the compilation *Crime Bites*.

- *Echo Rock* by Robert Daws
- *Old Dogs, Old Tricks* by AB Morgan
- *The Silence of the Rabbit* by Wendy Turbin
- *Never Mind the Baubles: An Anthology of Twisted Winter Tales* by the Hobeck Team (including many of the Hobeck authors and Hobeck's two publishers)
- *The Clarice Cliff Vase* by Linda Huber
- *Here She Lies* by Kerena Swan
- *Fatal Beginnings* by Brian Price
- *A Defining Moment* by Lin Le Versha
- *Saviour* by Jennie Ensor
- *You Can't Trust Anyone These Days* by Maureen Myant

Also please visit the Hobeck Books website for details of our other superb authors and their books, and if you would like to get in touch, we would love to hear from you.

Hobeck Books also presents a weekly podcast, the Hobcast, where founders Adrian Hobart and Rebecca Collins discuss all things book related, key issues from each week, including the ups and downs of running a creative business. Each episode includes an interview with one of the people who make Hobeck possible: the editors, the authors, the cover designers. These are the people who help Hobeck bring great stories to life. Without them, Hobeck wouldn't exist. The Hobcast can be listened to from all the usual platforms but it can also be found on the Hobeck website: **www.hobeck.net/hobcast**.

Finally, if you enjoyed this book, please also leave a review on the site you bought it from and spread the word. Reviews are hugely important to writers and they help other readers also.

ALSO BY MALCOLM HOLLINGDRAKE

Bridging the Gulf
A thriller set in Yorkshire and Cyprus

The Harrogate Crime Series
Only the Dead
Hell's Gate
Flesh Evidence
Game Point
Dying Art
Crossed Out
The Third Breath
Treble Clef
Threadbare
Fragments
Uncertainty of Reason
The Damascene Moment
Trapped Secrets
Past Promises

Also by Malcolm Hollingdrake

Short Story
'A Piece of Paper that Changed a Life' published in the charity
anthology, *Everyday Kindness*, edited by L. J. Ross